BROWATZKE

Parallel Lives

Rob Browatzke

BROWATZKE

Author's Foreword

This book is fiction. Mostly.

There was a little bar on 106 St in Edmonton called Boots, and in that bar, there were some princesses. A lot of fairy tales began and ended in that bar, and this is just one of them. Mostly.

Some of the names are changed; some of the stories are the same. But it's fiction. Mostly.

To the real princesses who inspired this mostly fiction, loads of love and lots of thanks, for everything.

BROWATZKE

PROLOGUE

It had been another long shift at the Underground, Edmonton's hottest bathhouse, and Michael was ready to be done. Sadly, there wasn't anyone doable currently checked in. It had been a while since he'd gotten off and Michael had been hoping that there'd be a hotty or two wandering about when he finally, well, got off.

But no.

He could always go to Divas. But it was a Tuesday. Not even the best dance club in the city was busy on Tuesdays. They had tried male strippers. They had tried Malebox nights. Nothing drew the guys out mid-week. And so it was cheap beer and free pool.

Michael didn't play free pool, but he did enjoy cheap beer. So Divas it would be, if this shift ever ended.

11:40.

11:45.

Oh, would this night never stop? And where was Nathaniel to take over the shift? If he was late again...

The buzzer went off, and Michael jumped to his feet, sure it was his shift relief. Guys' heads turned - they knew the buzzer meant potential fresh meat. Like Pavlov's dogs.

It was not Nathaniel. It was better than Nathaniel. Who was this

God? That's what this job was about, Michael thought, as he checked the guy in. Shawn, according to his ID. Dark curls and puppy dog eyes. Young, hung, and horny, just how Michael liked them. Well, hopefully hung. Not that he was a size queen.

As Michael handed Shawn the key to his locker, he made sure his fingers brushed the back of Shawn's hand. Their eyes met, and Michael felt the electricity, and he knew he had no competition on the floor. He was for sure the only other doable thing there tonight.

He watched Shawn head into the building, watched the other guys in the TV lounge watch Shawn head into the building. Sorry guys, he thought, this one is mine.

Michael amazed himself by how fast he managed to finish his cash-out, when Nathaniel finally did show up, at twenty after 12. Then it was out of the office, out of his clothes, into a towel, and into the hot tub before Puppy Dog Eyes even knew what was going on.

"Hey," Michael said.

Shawn opened his eyes, yes, there they were, those big brown bowls of puppy dog loving. He looked at Michael, and then closed them again.

What the...

"How's it going?" Michael asked, trying again.

Shawn sighed. "I'm just here to relax."

No one is here to relax, Michael thought. That was a no, plain and simple. What was he waiting for? It was a Tuesday. Did Little Mr. Brown Eyes really think someone better was going to come along? Maybe he was just new, and didn't know Michael was offering.

Third time's the charm, Michael thought. "I have a room."

"I have a headache."

Ouch.

Divas it was, Michael decided, and he was out of the tub, out of the towel, into his clothes, and into a cab before Nathaniel even realized he was gone.

The night was young, even if it was a Tuesday, and he was young, and there were a lot of guys with puppy dog eyes out there, waiting.

The next day, he stumbled into work, hungover. And nothing at Divas had been worth the hangover.

"You look like shit."

Michael looked across the counter to see who the endearment was coming from. George, of all people? George was a midday regular, old and fat and cranky. And in no position to judge anyone else's appearance.

"I feel like shit too."

"You kids don't know how to party."

"Oh, I think I do. I'm just hurting today, my head AND my wallet."

"Ha!" George slammed his hand down on the table. "If you want to play with the big dogs, you gotta be okay with getting bitten."

"What?" Michael asked. George had many expressions about big dogs, none of them that really made sense. "Look, old man, I don't have time for this today."

"Ha!" George slammed his fist down on the table again, laughing. "You have some spunk, kid. You looking for another job?"

"Why?"

"I need a bartender. This idiot last night decided to have a party after the bar closed. Came in today to find him passed out on the floor. I'm not a babysitter!"

"Bartender? Where at?"

"What? Don't you know who I am?"

"Yeah. You're Room 106. I have no clue who you are."

"They call me Gorgeous George. I own Choices."

"What's that?"

"Oh, you stupid kids. Think that Divas is all there is in this town. Choices has been around since before you were born, and those bitches like a bartender who can sass them back. Think you can handle that?"

"I can try. I've never bartended."

"What's in a rum and coke?"

"What?"

"I asked you a question!"

"Rum, and coke?"

"You're hired. You can start tomorrow."

 T hey called it the Princess Bar.

It was the first corner you came to when you walked in the door of Edmonton's oldest gay bar, Choices. Yes, pretty lame name. Maybe in 1969, when the bar opened, that name served as a beacon of sameness and welcome, but forty years later, it reeked of fromage. There were gay bars everywhere with names like Choices, Options, Alternatives... but Choices it had been christened in those glory days of gay rights in a just-post-Stonewall world, and Choices it remained, despite changes in ownership, membership, acceptance, openness...

When your entered the bar through its one-door, small-logo entrance, you saw a hallway leading to a horseshoe bar, and all the people sitting at that closest corner of the bar would turn their heads to see who was coming in. You might think it would've been less conspicuous to sit on the far corner, facing the door, but this was the Princess Bar. Inconspicuous ranked up there with discreet. They wanted to be seen noticing you, as much as many of the customers wanted to be noticed. "Oh fuck, you again?", "oh she survived last night I see", "speaking of cunts..." these were but some of the hellos that awaited you if you were in the chosen circle, if you too had earned a spot at the chosen corner.

At the Princess Bar.

All of this was presided over by two people. In a world where anyone could be a princess, these two were the queens.

One was the owner. He sat dead centre along that corner, and woe to him who usurped that spot. That was where he held court, where he both supervised the business he had spent years building, and where he got to party with his friends. After twenty plus years of Choices, and thirty plus years of "faggot bars" in total, he had earned the right, he said, to party with whom he chose: the other princesses of the Princess Bar. One of the reasons he was able to do this was because of the bartender, the other queen of the corner, who whether from natural instinct, or years of training, could also hold court, even as he dispensed pints of draft and shots of sambuca.

They were the Lord and Lady of the manor, the hosts of every party, the show that went with dinner. People came for the drinks and stayed for the fun. "You can never have just one" was an unofficial slogan of the Princess Bar. Even for newcomers, the constant banter, as evil and queeny as it sometimes became, was worth watching, and should that newcomer choose to join in... well, "don't dish out what you can't take" was number #2 on the list of unofficial slogans (a close third was "if you can't say anything nice, come sit by me" - and that always provoked a chuckle whenever Steel Magnolias was on cable).

There were no membership requirements for the Princess Bar, per se. Age, race, gender, job, these things didn't matter. Oh sure, the crowd was older than younger, and pretty white, and predominantly male, and mostly employed. They weren't the 18, 19, 20 year olds, graduating high school, coming out, losing themselves in the scene as bartenders, baristas, drag queens, waiters, hairdressers, whatever. Some, even many, had been at one point, but that was then. This was now.

"That was then. This was now" could've been an unofficial slogan. Could've, but wasn't, because too many of the Princess Bar Crew (the PBC) still clung to "that was then and then is still now". A 15 year old coming out was impossible. Gay marriage had been unlikely and for many was unnecessary and not understood, as was a new generation of homos so accustomed to the "exciting new treatments" and the "possible cures" for HIV that the death sentence the PBC had been forced to believe in was no more than the fear of blood tests and some injections to the little twinkies who occasionally crossed the doorstep.

Being gay was also not the be-all and end-all for the PBC. That didn't mean they were closeted at home or at work (though most had been). It just wasn't everything.

"Sucking dick or getting fucked doesn't obligate me to participate in any rally or parade. Fuck off, little political chicken. If it wasn't for old queens like us, you "we're so hard done by" gays would know what being hard done by really meant. Do your thing, more power to you, but am I going to go out of my way to sign this, protest that, and parade for the other? Honey I've done this, you go hard and let me know what happens, wanna sambuca?"

That is also an unrecorded unofficial slogan of the Princess Bar.

Being a member of the Princess Bar didn't mean you had to be old, white, male and employed.

It did mean you sure as hell better understand and respect what being old, white, male, employed, and gay meant in a city like Edmonton, and you sure as fuck better respect and appreciate how they got there.

Two queens held court.

One, the owner, who had lived it.

One, the bartender, who had lived it, vicariously.

Was it the same? No, and he knew that, appreciated that, accepted that, and everyone in the PBC knew that too. But he had put in the time and the effort to know why they mattered.

His name, this bartender, was Michael. Not Mike, and never Mikey. Michael. As in J. Fox, or Landon or Keaton or Row Your Fucking Boat Ashore.

Michael.

In a not-really out-of-the-way corner of downtown Edmonton,

one year after Dorothy went home for real real, not for play play, a bar called Choices opened. It was a members only liquor license. It was men only. It showed porn on the one TV, and played Diana Ross and Barbra Streisand on the stereo, and had a backroom in the back for, well, if you can't guess, you're reading the wrong book.

Eight years later, Michael was born, not too far away from that bar, as it turned out, and his nickname, given him by a doting mother and a proud father (who went by Mikey all the time, just sayin'), was Butch. Eighteen years later, that proud father was shacking up with a hot piece of tail called Ginger, the doting mother had also remarried, and that beloved son was anything but butch.

Michael wanted nothing more to get away from Edmonton and from family, and when time came to apply for colleges, he applied to the University of Lethbridge, five hours drive south, five hundred years south in acceptance of homosexuals, which Michael had known he was ever since, in Grade 3, his friend Kent had pulled out a Playboy and Michael had been far more interested in its effect on Kent than he had been on the presumably hot centerfold in question (years later, the likely fractured memory of Kent asking "hey buddy, gotta boner?" still automatically gave Michael a tent).

But the U of L, and the city surrounding it, was filled with Bible-thumping Christians and crazy-ass conservative Mormons, and the city clearly would have no gay life, but it was far away from Mom and new Dad and Dad and Dad's girlfriend. It was perfect for Michael.

Until he met Kevin Kosinski. Even years later, it was always Kevin Kosinski. Never just Kevin. Not even Kev, which is what Michael called him.

In Michael's head, it was always Kevin Kosinski.

The first guy he fell in love with.

And of course, Kevin Kosinski was straight.

Michael didn't know a soul in Lethbridge. That was part of his whole writing-them-out-of-his-life plan. He'd gone down in July, met a landlady who set up incoming freshmen with more senior students needing roommates. Michael knew he couldn't deal with dorm life.

Instead he ended up with Troy. Whose best friend was Kevin Kosinski. Who took a liking to the shy, quiet, kinda nelly Michael (complete opposite of the bold, brash, sexist, racist, misogynistic, homophobic Troy).

"Know why I like hanging around with you?" Kevin asked Michael one night as they were at the college pub for drinks.

"Honestly, no clue," Michael replied, choking on the words, choking on the hope.

"You're nothing like Troy and he's been my main man since like grade two."

"I know."

"But he drives off the hunnies. You must've seen it. He's just... an asshole sometimes, you know?"

As the pit under his heart grew bigger, Michael replied: "I hear ya, man. He totally is."

"Don't say shit man, cuz I am just drunk and venting but there's been too many times when we're out hunting for chicks and he totally blows it for me. It's never like that with you. When I start hitting on a chick, you pull back and let me score. That's what buds do man."

"Of course, man," Michael mumbled. "You'd do the same for me."

"Well, man, really, it's not likely to happen, is it? I mean we're not really anywhere you're gonna, well... you know..."

Michael didn't know. What was this? He'd never said, never hinted. He'd cruised the chicks on Melrose and Baywatch. He'd never indicated that it was like grade 3, that Troy's reaction, that Kevin's reaction, was way more interesting.

Had he?

"What?" was all he said.

"Shit dude, I'm bombed and it's late. I dunno what I'm saying."

"No. What did you mean?" Let it go, Michael, he told himself.

"Well, just that, I had the impression, well, I got the idea... well, I thought you were, like, well, like.. a fag, ya know?"

"What the fuck, dude? Why?"

"No, no, calm down. I don't care, man. I'm not Troy. But am I wrong?"

"Yah, fucking rights, asshole. You're totally wrong."

"Sorry dude, like I said, I'm bombed. I just thought, you never hook up... whatever man, maybe you should drive me home. I can't drive."

"Yah, you're wasted," Michael said, as coldly as possible.

"You're not though. Can you drive me home? I need my jeep in the morning. I'll pay for your cab from my place."

"I can't drive standard, dude. You know that."

"I'll tell you what to do. We'll go slow. I'll shift."

"I dunno man."

"Please, bud? I need my jeep there."

"Well..." Michael looked at Kevin's bleary, bloodshot, blue-green-gray-like-the-sky-before-a-storm eyes with his dimpled-have-there-ever-been-teeth-that-white smile...

"OK, so like your left foot's on the clutch right, so like let it up slowly as you slowly go down on the gas..."

After a few stalls, Michael's hands on the wheel, his feet on the pedals, with Kevin's hand shifting, they got moving. Michael was kinda excited. He'd only had his license less than a year, and he was pretty sure he'd be sober enough to remember this standard lesson tomorrow. And then he could drive Kevin home more often, and then...

They stalled again. "Sorry."

"S'all good, bro. Thanks for doing this."

They got going through the city, and Michael was getting the hang of it, and then they stopped at a set of lights. "Feel like shifting yourself?" Kevin Kosinski said.

As Michael hemmed and hawed, Kevin Kosinski took Michael's right hand off the wheel and put it on the gear shift.

"I don't..."

"I'll shift with you," was the reply. "let up the clutch as you slowly go down on the gas," Kevin Kosinski said as he moved Michael's hand on the gear shift.

There might've been more stalls. There might've been fuck-ups of all sorts. Feet moved up and down. Kevin Kosinski held Michael's hand as gears shifted up and down. And then... BAM.

"Well, here's my place. Thanks bud." It was Kevin Kosinski's driveway, already. Michael didn't even remember pulling into it. "You OK, bud?"

"Uhm... yah... wow... I just don't all of a sudden feel as sober as I thought."

"Shitty, dude. I'd say crash here but my roomie has a friend from out of town on the couch."

"S'all good man. I'm OK."

"You can sleep on the floor in my room if you want."

Michael's head (et cetera) lit up like New Year's Eve. "Fuck man maybe that's for the best. I'm feeling pretty wasted."

Five minutes later.

On the floor in Kevin Kosinski's bedroom.

"That blanket enough, man?"

"Sh-sh-sh-sure, it's all, g-g-g-good, man." The stuttering was only semi-faked.

"Fuck, dude, I forgot how cold it can get on these cement floors. Cheap shitty thin carpet. You gotta blanket, you can crash up here if you want.

Crash Up Here.

If You Want.

Says Kevin Kosinski.

From His Bed.

"Well.. if you're sure you don't mind..."

"Fuck, dude, just do it. I'm passing out... all those shots..."

Climbing into Kevin Kosinski's bed without touching him was the hardest thing Michael had ever done.

But it was warmer.

No surprise.

It's so dark, he thought. He's so close. I'm so drunk. So tired. Ah fuck, I have an ANTHRO midterm at 9.

Kevin Kosinski's back was towards him.

Kevin Kosinski was snoring.

It's accidental, right? Michael asked himself. People cuddle in their sleep.

His hand crept forward.

Shoulder.

Pec.

Bare Pec.

Hard Muscly Bare Pec.

Rippled Ab.

Rippled Ab.

Rippled Ab.

Waistband of underwear.

Kevin Kosinski was still snoring.

Fingers left waistband, hovered downwards, pulled back, moved downwards, grazed something not entirely soft, pulled back, paused.

Waistband of underwear.

Fingers pried up, reached something less entirely soft.

Rested on it.

On him.

Kevin Kosinski.

Fingers circled it entirely.

Michael's lips touched Kevin Kosinski's back.

One little (not so little) stroke.

The snoring stopped.

Kevin Kosinski rolled onto his back as Michael's hands returned to their proper place.

Michael felt Kevin Kosinski lift off the bed as he slid his underwear down.

Kevin Kosinski took Michael's head and gently oh so gently forced it down into his lap, onto that hard beautiful swelling masculine throbbing that awaited.

"Don't tell Troy," Kevin Kosinski said.

Michael, his mouth, head, heart full, had no idea who Troy was.

The Princess Bar welcomes everyone.

Kind of.

When it comes to first-time experiences, they have seen it all. Young, nelly, faggy, old, butch, married, closeted, open, backroom, bathhouse, park, and now internet.

Internet killed the gay bar, the bathhouse.

If Video felt guilty for the Radio Star, then the Internet should be doubling over in grief.

The PBC remembers when gay bars were almost impossible to find. When even hanky codes didn't exist.

The PBC remembers where if you were gay and wanted action, that's where you went.

The PBC finds it hard to understand a world of sexually-active, socially-out-there politically-acceptable homosexuals who can come out, hook up, marry off, and never set foot in a gay bar.

Even amongst themselves, friends and family as they are to each other, those relationships began in hooking up. They grew stronger in fighting together. They got tested (and tested and tested and finally passed) by a virus that ate away at their own. They lost friends, lovers, family, until at times it seemed that their lives were more 4 Funerals and a Wedding than the other way around.. but surviving counted for something.

Counted for a lot.

It wasn't a moral judgment. They weren't better than the friends they'd lost. And god knows it wasn't a political or medical judgment because the straights started getting it too.

It was luck. Kinda. And learning. A lot. And life. Even more.

It was there.

Always.

Not the gay cancer, but like a cancer.

HIV was like the Princess Bar. It had no membership requirements, per se. Age, race, gender, job, sexual orientation, these things didn't matter.

On one side of the Princess Bar, you had Statler and Waldorf, two guys well into their 70s, who had been at Choices opening day, who had had years of casual, indiscriminate, eventually unsafe sex, who, there-but-for-the-grace-of-God-go-them, were negative. Clean. Uninfected if never unaffected.

Also at the Princess Bar, you had Matt and Jonny, two 20-year-olds who came out together at 16, in high school, as boyfriends, never had sex with anyone but each other in their 4 years, but still used condoms every time because it's 2013 and unsafe sex is anything other than jerking off in a bubble.

Barebacking, unsympathizing, apparently-invincible fags shouldn't even apply for the PBC.

Death, loss, grief, they are life's great equalizers. You can't appreciate life until you've been forced to face death.

And the closet is a great place to be safe until you've tasted freedom.

Kevin Kosinski was gone when Michael woke up but it was like he was Black in 1863 Georgia. The fact that he was a History major with a Gone with the Wind obsession definitely factored into his early morning metaphors, but the point was, he was free.

He had known it, deep, underneath, but it was Kevin Kosinski who named it and brought it forth.

Michael Collins was a homosexual. Gay. A fag.

And he was in love.

With his homophobic roommate's supposedly heterosexual best friend Kevin Kosinski.

And he was living in the Bible Belt of Alberta, where Christian fundamentalism was a way of life in the form of Christ Jesus is Lord Television. In this city of 65,000, there were no gay bars, no gay.... where else did gay guys go? There were no gays.

But who needed other gays?

Michael had Kevin Kosinski.

"Hey Kev, it's Michael. Call me when you get home." BEEP.

"Hey bud, it's Michael again. Had a blast last night, whatcha doin later? Call me." BEEP.

"Well, it's like 9:00, time to hit the bars, hey Kev? Troy's not going out tonight but we can totally do something if you want. I have no exams or classes tomorrow. Maybe another driving lesson? Call me. I'll be up for a bit. It's Michael, by the way." BEEP.

Tuesday became Wednesday, which became Thursday, which became Friday, which became the following Friday before Michael even realized and Kevin Kosinski came over to watch the game with Troy.

Michael hated hockey. It reminded him of a dad he barely knew and a step-dad he couldn't love.

Kevin Kosinski loved hockey.

"I hope the Oilers make the play offs," Michael offered.

"Yah you would." Troy sneered as he said it. "Flames all the way." Kevin Kosinski snickered.

Michael felt flames on his face but didn't stop. "Well, we're not the City of Champions for nothing. Between the Oilers and the Esks, we kick Calgary's butt." Gay or not, you didn't grow up in Edmonton without being infected with an anti-Calgary bias.

"Michael, can you name one year the Oilers won the Cup? Or the

Eskimos?" Kevin's smile was mocking, moreso when Michael turned beat red. Troy laughed and chugged back the last of his beer and went to piss.

"Uhm, Kev..."

"Look dude, shut up already. I was drunk. I'm not a fag. The bitches had just been so teasy and I knew you wanted it. It was a one time thing and I wish it didn't happen." It was delivered so fast, felt so rehearsed, and Michael felt his heart hit his feet.

"But..."

"No buts. Shut the fuck up about it. Don't make me tell Troy he's living with a fucking cocksucker."

"No, no, don't do that..."

"...cuz he already thinks you are."

"I'm not! It was that one time..."

"Then leave it that one time... actually, I'm pretty sure you should be studying in your room and leave hockey for us men."

It was a dismissal, and Michael took it as such. He lay in his room, hearing Troy and Kevin Kosinski laugh, swear, whatever. He remembered Kevin Kosinski's soft warm skin. He heard Kevin Kosinski call a non-scoring player a fucking faggot. He tasted Kevin Kosinski's sweet-salty load. His chest tightened as he realized he was just a stupid drunken faggot in Kevin Kosinski's eyes.

But he was a faggot.

He knew that now.

And neither split-up parents, Lethbridge fundamentalists, homophobic roommates called Troy nor beautiful heterosexuals like Kevin Kosinski could make him forget that moment of rightness, of completeness, that he'd felt when his skin first touched Kevin Kosinski's.

At the Princess Bar, sex was, if not #1, high up on the list of conversation. Who wanted who. Who's doing who. Who's done who.

If everybody knew your name at Cheers, at the Princess Bar, everybody knew your name and everything else.

When you grow up together, such intimacy doesn't matter. Even catty jealousy can contain congratulations. A social circle that had evolved beyond sex, even if it began, partly, with sex, is bitter when friends in the circle go outside of it. Even if they know they always come back. They want every juicy detail because they are living through their friends. How big was he? How smooth? A top, a bottom? Cut or uncut? What did you say about chocolate? Really? All over you? He let you shower after, I hope? Goddam, you're a whore.

To which the response is invariably one of two things:

Jealous much?

Or...

Whores charge, and who's gonna pay for what I can't even give away?

The latter has truth. The PBC don't have a lot of sex. Oh they have, in the past, been there, done that, used the T-shirt to wipe it up.

The former also has truth. When one of the PBC hooks up, they break the circle. For one moment, one night, one week, however long the hook-up lasts, they are free from the routine. The routine of daily happy hour pints of draft, shots of sambuca, bitchy if friendly commentary, and turning heads.

Heads turn because the next one through the door could be their ticket to freedom. If only for the moment, the night, the week...

Which just goes to show any 50-year-old-Princess can get just as giddy as any 19-year-old-just-coming-out-homo when it comes to that first taste of freedom.

Fine! Michael thought when he woke up the next morning with a piss-hard boner about, surprisingly, Troy, not Kevin Kosinski. Fine! Kevin Kosinski doesn't want me but someone will. It might not be Edmonton or Calgary but 65,000 people... there's gotta be more gay ones.

A quick search through the phone book had him thrilled.... a Gay and Lesbian Peer Support Line... he didn't feel he needed any peer support but he definitely felt he needed to feel some gay peers.

"Gay and Lesbian Peer Support Line. My name is Robert, how can I help you?"

Michael hung up. The guy, that Robert, he just sounded like a fag. Well... beggars can't be choosy, can they Butch? he asked himself.

"Gay and Lesbian Peer Support Line. My name is Robert, how can I help you?"

"Uhm... yah uhm hi, my name's Michael, and I think, well, I know, that I'm, that is I'm pretty sure I'm... I'm gay."

Saying that, admitting that, in a way, it was even better than Kevin Kosinski's penis in his mouth. And the guy, that Robert, didn't judge, deny, contradict, nothing. He accepted, moved on, wanted to listen. He cared!

By the end of the 20-minute conversation, the guy, that Robert, didn't sound so faggy.

By the end of the 20-minute conversation, Michael had also agreed to meet the guy, that Robert, at "their" weekly coffee night. The guy, that Robert, would be in jeans and an orange CM sweatshirt. He would be expecting Michael at 7:00.

By Monday, Michael had decided he wasn't going to go. What had happened with Kevin Kosinski was a fluke, and he was drunk, and the right girl was out there, somewhere.

Tuesday, Troy made about 27 more fag jokes than usual, and Kevin Kosinski laughed at every one. Whether the punchline was Mega-sore-ass or Roll-AIDS, faggot or not, Michael was offended.

Wednesday, well, Wednesday was the day before Thursday, and Thursday, well, that was the day Michael went to Gay Coffee in Conservative Lethbridge, and that was the night Michael realized that being gay doesn't mean shit.

The first time he heard the voice of the guy, that Robert, he pictured him as limp-wristed, effeminate, wanting to be a woman. He'd seen Priscilla. He'd seen Melrose. Fags were pussies.

But...

The guy, that Robert, listened, and as he listened, he got less nelly, less old, less fat, more blond, more tanned, more toned, basically, the guy, that Robert, became Kevin Kosinski.

With a super gay voice.

Gay Coffee Night in Lethbridge was held on Thursdays from 8-10 at a downtown coffee place called "Cravings". It wasn't a "gays-only" place; Lethbridge didn't have those. But there was a backroom (and it was years later before Michael got that irony) where the gays could meet. On Thursdays. From 8-10.

But Robert (no longer the guy, no longer that Robert) was to meet Michael at 7. And Michael had his gay-version-of-Kevin-Kosinski / Matt-from-Melrose-but-with-abs image in his head.

The only orange CM sweatshirt was being worn by a balding, bearded, pushing-40, glasses-wearing clear homosexual.

Michael was about to walk out when...

"Michael?" the guy, that Robert, called.

Whatever, Michael thought. "Yes." And he sat down.

"I'm not what you thought."

It wasn't a question; it still got answered. "No."

"You pictured a hot college jock, maybe someone you know, someone you wanted to be gay."

"How did you..."

"I'm old. Live and learn."

"Sorry. I just..."

"You just wanted to come out and meet another gay guy and ride off into the sunset and happily ever after the end."

Michael smiled. "Pretty much."

"Life's not a fairy tale, Michael," the guy, that Robert, said. "Especially for us fairies," he added with a smirk.

Michael chuckled nervously. "How long have you been..." What did he say? Fag felt wrong. Gay felt accepting. Homosexual felt too... But Robert understood.

"Gay? Always. But I've been out for 15 years."

"Here?"

"Here."

"Wow. How? Your family?"

"It wasn't easy. It took time. It's not perfect, but it's better."

"But why wouldn't you move? To like Vancouver or Toronto or...?"

"You think it's easier there? Being gay, coming out, it's hard wherever... some places just make the after part easier."

"So why didn't you move?"

"My family's here, my friends. My job. That's a lot to give up for gay bars and rainbow flags."

"But isn't it, like, lonely? How do you meet people? People that are like... you?"

"Don't you mean like us? You'll see in half an hour or so Michael, if you choose to stay. Even here, you can be gay, be accepted. Just like anywhere else though, being accepted has to start with yourself."

Years later, comparing the stories he heard around the Princess Bar, Michael knew he'd never compare their coming outs in the 60s, 70s, 80s, to his own, but he realized that when all is said and done, any year, any age, any city, the guy, that Robert, was right.

The first person you need to come out to is you.

By 8:30 on That Thursday, the backroom of that Lethbridge coffee shop was full. Big fat lesbians. Stereotypically nelly faggots. And a bunch of men and women in the middle. They sat together, drank their coffee, shared their weeks. Like a straight family at dinner in a bad TGIF sitcom. The 'gay' was there, but almost incidentally.

Michael sat, watched, learned, remembered.

They were younger, older, richer, poorer, new-at-it, old hacks, students, employed, married, single, political, indifferent. Some were hot, some were not, but that Thursday in that backroom, Michael realized they all had something he didn't have. Honesty? Integrity? Self-respect? He didn't know the word, then, but he knew he needed it, and it was more important that sucking all the Kevin Kosinski cocks he could find.

It wasn't HIM.

But it was a part of him.

A big part.

And he owed it to himself to let that part out.

There was a table with three or four people his age, currently at a lull in conversation,

There was an empty chair.

"Hi, I'm new here," he said as he sat down. "My name's Michael. Mind if I join you?"

The Princess Bar welcomed newcomers, but it seemed at times that they required that same nerve, that same initiative that Michael showed That First Thursday. Otherwise, you sat there, watching, listening. Sometimes that's what it took.

Four years after That First Thursday, Michael convocated and moved home. The reasons he'd had to move away didn't seem so big now. Even though for an out and proud gay man in Lethbridge, Calgary was the closer oasis, Edmonton was home. When Michael moved home, in spite of his degree, he wanted to reestablish the acceptance and the popularity he'd found in Lethbridge. From New Fag on the Block, he's gone on to become Someone in the gay community. People knew him, liked him. High school hadn't been like that. Gay life was. In a small pool, he'd been a big fish. He wanted that in Edmonton.

So, degree or not, when he moved home, his first decision was to get a job "somewhere gay", and the Edmonton Rainbow Business Association directory was the tool he used. Resumes went off, one by one, bars, bathhouses, coffee shops, magazine stores, restaurants... his Bachelor of Arts demonstrated a willingness to learn if nothing else.

It was a bathhouse that first snapped him up.

And that temporary job became a turning point for the rest of his life. In four years, he'd gone from a quiet nerdy high school graduate to closeted cock-sucking university freshman, to out of the closet homosexual in Alberta's most conservative basket, to over-the-top out-of-the-closet politically-homosexual hardcore-faggot-with-a-degree to towel bitch at Edmonton's bathhouse, the Underground.

Michael was born in 1977.

Michael was in Grade 4 in 1986 when he had his first sex ed class, and that was the first year when AIDS was a topic to be taught.

"Gay" was barely, rarely, never mentioned.

"Bathhouse" surely wasn't.

Michael's experience of bathhouses was profoundly different than the other opinions he heard around the Princess Bar. In a different era, an era of closets, of codes, of camp, an era that was pre-HIV, the bathhouse was, in many ways, a direct alternative to cruising the bars. You went in, paid your money, took your chances. It was about sex. The bars were too, but less directly. Then along came this new gay cancer, which turned out not to be divine wrath but sexually transmitted, and some studies came along linking new infections of this new disease to the baths, and that led to bathhouses closing. There was a generation then, that Michael ended up knowing, loving, serving pints of draft and shots of sambuca to, that saw baths as directly linked to casual sex and therefore, directly linked to HIV and other STIs.

Michael had been to bathhouses before getting a job at the Underground, but it had been for those direct casual sex kind of purposes.

As an employee of a bathhouse at the turn of the century, he saw a very different kind of business than he saw in films like And The Band Played On or read about in books like Tales of the City.

In spite of his personal experiences, the PBC didn't believe him. Even though age wasn't a barrier for the PBC, a generation gap still existed. Like in marriage, baths, safer sex, HIV, gay bars, coming out, the Internet, icons, queens, dykes, bisexuals, casual sex, et cetera.

Big societies go through major cultural changes slowly and gradually. Small societies, not so much. Think of the PBC as French nobility in 1792, as American plantation owners in 1863. Rules change; practice takes longer.

Gay couples that spent 40 years together without a government-issued license may find it hard to understand why many people find it such an issue.

A generation that lost half of itself to a horrible disease may have difficulty accepting why an even-more educated younger generation can go about practicing practices that killed so many friends and lovers, thereby giving longevity to a virus that didn't need any help.

When drag queens and trannies are, ironically, the only ones with balls big enough to challenge blatant discrimination, it's hard for the people that remember Stonewall to swallow the current "They don't represent all of gays" anti-drag/tranny diatribes that surface so constantly. In those days after Judy Garland died, they remember a distinct lack of realtors, accountants, doctors out challenging the NYPD.

There was a time when, to meet gay men, gay men had to go to gay bars. But then BAM! Along comes this Internet thing. Why dress up, go out, et cetera, to cruise? Do so from the privacy of your own laptop, where emailed .jpgs show you (maybe) what you're gonna get, where there's no last call, no closet, no "gay" other than sucking cock.

Add onto that increased acceptance of homos in the mainstream with Roseanne and Rosie and Ellen and Elton and every sitcom's token gay, and small wonder the PBC found their beloved gay bar had become a dinosaur, stumbling about to passé divas like Cher and Madonna, struggling to create new icons in Britney and Gaga, while offering the same out-of-the-way locations, dark and unmarked, that they always have.

Even as it destroyed personal interaction, dating, the awkwardness of cruising, the necessity of going/coming, the Internet destroyed the Gay Bar and Baths scene in a way Video never hoped to do to the Radio Star.

And the PBC knew that.

That's why the younger members they "allowed" needed to understand that, even as that injection of new young blood kept the PBC current with texting and Manhunt and Facebook and Choicesbar.ca...

The PBC didn't go out to cruise, and the reason that the corner became inviting and acceptable to newbies / chicken / twinkies / fresh meat was that even the "dirty old men" they expected on walking into Choices, no matter how lewd or inappropriate their comments, were not pedophiles taking advantage of anything. It was a symbiotic relationship. The younger generation got guidance, advice, experience (all too often ignored because, as the PBC knew, the best lessons are those you learn yourself). The older generation got a connection to the new world, a world their labor pains gave birth to, a world they never thought to see.

When Michael left the 98% heterosexual cruising world of Lethbridge, he wanted to embrace, 100%, the part of him he had learned to accept and love.

Working at the Underground started that.

Meeting one of the regulars there, the in-your-face-to-the-point-you'd-like-to-smack-him George, who happened to own Choices, enabled Michael to finish it.

When Michael, with George, first set foot in Choices, he met the people of the Princess Bar.

Within moments, he knew his life was changed, improved, forever.

It took the PBC a bit longer.

But eventually, they knew the same.

That First Thursday Night changed Michael forever. He was out now, for one. OK, sure, not to his family, friends, or anyone that knew him, but he was out. To himself. And that mattered a helluva lot more than he thought it would.

And That First Thursday Night, Michael did not, as he hoped, meet the man of his dreams. Even just as friends, he didn't really make a connection. But he met people. Gay people. That made all the difference. This 'thing' about him, this 'thing' he now knew he'd always known but never really knew, this 'thing' wasn't unique to him.

Even in the anti-gay conservative back-ass wards end of a big anti-gay conservative back-ass wards province of Canada, Michael Collins wasn't alone.

Still, he didn't go back right away.

But everything was changed.

When Troy or Kevin Kosinski made the little gay jokes, he tensed up, or got mad.

The more he tensed, the more they made.

The madder he got, the more they made about him.

But still, Troy and Kevin Kosinski were like his only friends. And about two months after That First Thursday Night, it was the three of them, at the local college bar, drinking like always.

"Fuck dudes, I'm smashed, I need to crash." It was Troy saying it, Michael interpreted through his drunken stupor. "You comin' Mikey?" he added.

"Michael," Kevin Kosinski started, emphasizing the name, "and I will finish our drinks at least. We're trying to land some pussy." Kevin Kosinski loved his pussy.

"Whatever, faggots," Troy slurred as he stumbled off.

And there it was.

For the first time since, well, since that First Time, Michael was alone with Kevin Kosinski.

"I'm pretty smashed too," Michael said, not knowing, not caring, wanting to avoid. "Maybe I should head 'er too."

"You're not that smashed, dude. At least let's have one more pint and see if one of us can't snag that hot waitress. Fuck, she's got a sweet rack."

"I really don't..."

All of a sudden there was a hand on Michael's knee.

Kevin Kosinski's hand.

"Sure you don't want just one more?" The suggestive smile that lit up his face in dimples was as gorgeous as the normal smile that lit up his face in dimples. Michael caved.

Thirty minutes later.

"I need my jeep in the morning. Think you can remember how to shift stick?" Was the innuendo only in Michael's brain? Did he care?"

"I..."

"C'mon bud. Sorry I razzed you about last time. I promise. Just get my jeep home with me in it."

"Well... ok.."

After four stalls in two blocks, Kevin Kosinski put his hand on Michael's hand on the stick shift and shifted for him, with him, as he told Michael again how and when to move his feet. When they pulled up to Kevin Kosinski's house, Michael killed the engine, pulled on the park brake and opened the door.

Kevin Kosinski grabbed his hand.

Michael looked at him. He was drunk. They were both drunk. Anything was a mistake.

"You can crash here if you want."

"I should cab home."

"No one's here. No biggie."

"I should cab home."

Kevin Kosinski grabbed his hand but didn't guide it to the gear shift this time. "Please buddy?" The gear shift may have been softer.

"You treated me like crap," Michael said, not moving his hand. Through khakis, he could feel every throb. "Why should I..."

Kevin Kosinski leaned over the gear shift and kissed Michael hard on the lips. Then pulled away. "I'm not a fucking fag," he said, looking Michael square in the eyes.

Kevin Kosinski didn't break eye contact as his hand slowly undid Michael's zipper.

Michael's heart relocated to his throat.

Kevin Kosinski went down on Michael right there in his jeep.

Fucking fag or not, Michael spent the night.

"...and so, fucking fag or not, I totally spent the night," Michael said. "And let me tell you, it's a pity I didn't know what rimming was back then because goddam, he had a sweet fucking ass!" There were appreciative chuckles around the Princess Bar. "Not as sweet as yours though Jonny." The chuckles became laughs. "Oh fuck, it's her," Michael exclaimed as the door opened. "Little Buddy Pump herself."

PBC heads turned to greet Little Buddy Pump (LBP for short), so named because he bore a striking resemblance to Gilligan and loved to get pumped.

"I thought we'd reached our quota for cunts," Michael said.

"Just remember," LBP replied, "you can't spell CUNT without U."

As the PBC laughed, Michael poured LBP his usual Rum and Diet. "So... tell us a story."

"Oh you should've seen the dark chocolate I had over last night. A sweet black daddy."

"Where do you find these men?"

"I have my sources, and I'm not sharing! I can mow my own grass, thank you very much!"

"You can have one of our seats, Little Buddy," Matt said, as he and Jonny got up to leave. "We both work early so we're done for the night."

"Awww really?" Michael said with a pout. "Who am I going to cruise?" The constant flirtation between Michael and Jonny was an ongoing joke at the Princess Bar, especially since everyone knew it was Matt that Michael really preferred. Not that he'd say no to Jonny. Or both.

Michael started to clean up Matt and Jonny's drinks to make room for Little Buddy when Jonny reached out to grab his glass. "Uhm, hello, I am not done with that. There's still beer n there."

Michael held up the glass with its last few drops. "What? That little bit of backwash? Okay... I guess there's kids in Ethiopia that can't even afford warm beer spit."

The PBC laughed. Michael grinned, and started to pour another round of sambuca.

A few minutes later, another of the Princesses, Darcy (Iona in drag), caught Michael's eye with a subtle jerk of the head. Michael replied with a barely perceptible nod. Within the minute, Michael and Darcy met in stall #2 of the ladies washroom, Darcy straddling the toilet as he busted out two lines of coke, Iona-sized, as he called them. He rolled the twenty he'd used to crush them and handed it to Michael. Michael snorted back his, then Darcy went.

"Am I good?" Michael asked, offering his nose for VCR (visual coke residue) inspection.

"Yah. Me?"

"Yah."

"Thanks."

"No, thank you!" Michael grinned. One last sniff, then out of the bathroom. "All right bitches, whose turn is it to buy shots?"

In about twenty seconds, Michael was flying. Pints and jokes got dispensed freer and faster. Drugs at the Princess Bar, other than pot, were ignored by those not using. Not approved, not disapproved, just conveniently ignored.

"OK!" George barked from his stool. "Round of sambuca! Then I want to see you lay it on the bar!" The first was to Michael; the second was to Adam, one of the young pretty-boys that had taken to hanging out at Choices as an alternative to the Stand-and-Model Pose-and-Preen thump thump thump dance clubs. "I'll buy you a drink for every inch," George said, then slammed his hand on the bar. "Ha! You'll owe me money!" He laughed. "Or you can dance on the bar and give these old bitches a thrill!"

The PBC laughed and clapped, but to no avail. Adam blushed as George grabbed his crotch, squealing with delight. But Adam wasn't up to dancing on the bar.

Yet.

"More sambuca!" George barked.

Having absolutely no aversions to seeing Adam naked on the bar, Michael rushed to comply.

Michael never saw Kevin Kosinski again after that night but the feelings of sweaty bodies intertwining, of warm wet mouths, hot roaming hands, tension building, building, building and then BAM! Sticky sweet freedom, those feelings, if nothing else, sent him back to those Gay Coffee Nights in search of someone to feel them with again.

It was a couple months after that First Thursday Night when Michael met Troy. It wasn't Troy's first Gay Coffee Night but it was his first in a while. Troy was 27, and beautiful. A pilot. A god.

Michael made eye contact.

Troy smiled.

Michael fell in love.

Troy ordered his coffee.

Michael's eyes wandered up and down Troy's figure, the chestnut hair hanging onto his shoulders, his broad shoulders, the way his jeans clung to his butt, to his thighs. 6 feet 2 inches of masculine perfection.

Michael couldn't, of course, actually talk to this perfection.

The next Gay Coffee Night, Michael met Troy's new boyfriend, and he finally understood Alanis' 'Ironic'. He also learned a valuable lesson about grabbing the horny bull by the horns.

He also learned that when you get drunk to cope with your crush having a new boyfriend, you can end up waking up next to someone you don't remember going home with.

That was how Michael met Wayne.

Not too pretty. Not too smart. But he'd been there, apparently, and, apparently, physical contact trumped sexual attraction.

Apparently.

Sometimes.

"So uhm, Wayne, about last night..." Michael paused, unsure how to say something he didn't even know what it was.

"It's fine man," Wayne yawned, sitting up in bed. "We were both drunk. It happens."

Michael laughed nervously. "I really don't even remember how it happened."

"Well a bunch of us went to 'Stangs after coffee."

"Yah I remember that."

"And a bunch of us were dancing, and doing shots, and you walked me home, and I invited you in, and, well..."

"Yah, I don't remember a fucking thing. Were we safe?"

"We didn't really do anything. Some oral. Neither of us were really into it."

"K, well, I should get going. I have class at noon, and, uhm, Wayne, it'd be cool if this was just between us."

"Yah, no problem dude. Our secret."

Michael went to Gay Coffee the next Thursday and the first thing he heard was "so, you and Wayne hey?"

So much for secrets.

"**W**ell here comes trouble!" George yelled as Princess Sophia Maria Victoria Secret walked into the bar. His real name was Rick, and he was so incredibly furry and butch that calling him Princess Sophia Maria Victoria Secret was beyond ridiculous.

"You don't know the half of it," Michael smirked.

"Shut up!" Princess Sophia yelled.

"Oooh gossip!" LBP perked up for any and all juicy tidbits.

"You wouldn't believe who Rick went home from Divas with last night."

"Shut up, I said!"

"Who signs your paycheck, Michael? Me or Princess there? Who did he do?"

"Well, I did promise not to say but let's just say the guy just moved here, and Rick was probably horny again in thirty minutes."

"Ho Chi Minh!" George yelled, slapping the bar.

"His name is William," Rick said defensively, as the PBC laughed.

William had just moved from Vancouver, and although he was Chinese, his poor English had earned him the nickname Ho Chi Minh. To George anyway.

And everyone knew Rick was a rice queen.

"He sucka you peepee long time? Five dolla make you holla?" Darcy asked.

"You've got a big fucking mouth, Michael," Rick said.

"Hey buddy, don't make out in a bar if you don't want the dirt dished. Besides, at least you're getting some. That's more than these hookers. Or me for that matter. I haven't had sex in so long even LBP is starting to look good." Michael paused. "That could be the sambuca though."

"Oh go lay by your dish," LBP came back with as the PBC laughed.

At Choices, Happy Hour was from 4-8.

Bitchy Hour was all day long.

By the end of Michael's first year of University, he had changed majors, changed apartments to avoid the increasingly homophobic Troy (how could such an asshole share a name with such a hotty?), and changed from being single to being happily hitched.

The boyfriend's name was David. Not Dave or Davey.

Which was Point One in his favor.

He was also fairly newly out and had never had a boyfriend.

Which was Point Two in his favor.

And, he had asked Michael out.

Which was the telling point.

They had met at one of the monthly gay dances, and clicked. They exchanged numbers, went for a couple movies, out for coffee, dinner. Neither of them wanted to rush into anything. Michael was still borderline-obsessed with Troy (hotty pilot not asshole roomie) and David, well, David was still completely a virgin.

Michael wore his few experiences with pride. None had been fabulous, but all had been his.

It was after their fourth movie date, while Michael was walking David home, when David stopped and turned to face Michael. "Do you want to be boyfriends?" he blurted, then blushed. "That sounded cooler in my head."

Michael looked David in the eyes and leaned in to kiss him. Firmly. When he pulled away, he asked, "does that answer your question?"

David's grin matched Michael's as they finished the walk to David's.

"Do you want to come up?"

"Do you want me to come up?"

"I do if you want to come up."

"Well, I do if you do," Michael said, being deliberately though playfully difficult.

"Can I just please get naked with you?"

David's directness floored Michael for a moment, but then in the frantic kissing, undressing, groping that followed, Michael found what had been lacking with Kevin, with Wayne.

Two bodies. In sync.

Ironically sound-tracked by the Backstreet Boys.

David and Michael dated for nearly a year of delirious happiness. Happiness, because the sex was amazing. Delirious, because they were partying so much with the gay crew at 'Stangs that the nights became a blur and the mornings became a dry-mouthed, aching-head, queasy-stomached attempt to put the pieces back together.

The break-up, when it happened, was a strange mirror image of the night it had begun. They were at Michael's after a night of dancing, the tequila shot still warming their blood as they crawled into bed. David rolled onto Michael and started kissing him. It just felt wrong to Michael, the spark had fizzled. He was... bored...

David could tell something was off. He pulled back. "What's wrong?"

"I dunno. Just not in the mood I guess."

"You've been not in the mood a lot lately."

"Don't start, Dave," Michael said, emphasizing the name.

"Don't call me Dave, Mikey," David snapped back. "Is this about Troy?"

"Oh for fuck sakes, David. Just because him and Cory finally broke up..."

"...which you've been waiting for..."

"...doesn't mean I'm all in love with him again."

"Again. You never even fucked much less dated. You barely know him."

"That's not what I meant."

"I think it is."

"Can we not do this?"

"OK, we won't fuck, we won't fight, let's just sleep."

David rolled onto his side. Michael looked at the tenseness in his back and shoulders and knew David was partly right. Ever since

Troy and Cory had broken up, he was obsessed with him again. He loved David, he was sure he did, probably, but this was Troy. Troy! It could be better. But he felt so guilty about hurting David.

He put his arm around David and kissed his shoulder. "I'm sorry. I love you." He slid his hand down to David's hips.

Two bodies. Out of sync.

Still ironically sound-tracked to the Backstreet Boys.

The next morning, Michael looked at David in the eyes and said "can we talk?"

"Can we talk?" Jonny asked Michael.

"Sure man." Michael had just opened the bar. Even George wasn't there yet. Just Michael and Jonny-with-the-hot-ass-and-hotter-boyfriend. "What's up?"

"Fuck man, I think I wanna break up with Matt."

"Wow dude, why? I thought things were going so well."

"It was, well, it is, but it's been four years. I'm just..."

"Bored?"

"I dunno. Maybe. I guess that's it. The sex is still unbelievably hot, but it's just everything else, you know?"

"Like what?"

"Well, it's like every day is the same thing. Get up, work, come here for happy hour, have dinner, watch TV, fuck, sleep. Lather, rinse, repeat."

"You know, that sounds not bad to me," Michael said in all honesty. "There's lotsa guys I know who'd love just that comfort and consistency."

"Well good for them then. I just keep thinking, there could be, like, more, you know?"

Michael thought of that long ago first boyfriend. "Is there someone else?"

"No no, it's nothing like that. Well, of course there's other guys that I think are hot, but there's no one specific." Jonny paused. "Well, not really." Jonny's eyes met Michael's. The door opened.

"Let's get this party started," George yelled as he marched up and took his place at the Princess Bar.

"Don't say anything," Jonny whispered.

"Sambucas?" Michael asked George and Jonny. The door opened and more of the PBC walked in.

So Jonny wasn't happy, Michael thought. That would mean Matt was free. And that look in Jonny's eyes... did he want me?

It could be a Very Happy Happy Hour at the Princess Bar.

For two out of three anyway.

When Matt arrived for his post-work gin-and-tonic, Jonny tipped back his beer. "Hey babe, I'm starving, can we just go?" he said as he hugged Matt.

"Sure I guess," he giggled, "see you guys tomorrow."

"Yah, bye guys," Jonny said, pulling Matt down the hallway back to the door.

"Bye, you two," LBP said with a wink.

"Yah, we all know what Jonny's really hungry for," Darcy added.

Jonny's eyes met Michael's, pleading him for silence. "Night you two, see you tomorrow," Michael grinned.

"What's going on there?" George asked.

"Nothing, far as I know," Michael lied. "You know, sometimes hungry can just mean hungry."

"You just don't want to think about Jonny tapping Matt's ass," LBP said.

Everyone laughed and Michael grinned too, even as he pictured Jonny tapping Matt's ass. And Michael wasn't sure which ass he enjoyed picturing more.

"What's with your dreamy grin?" LBP asked.

"Just thinking happy thoughts."

"Any merry little thought?" Darcy joked.

"Fuck you're gay," Michael laughed, as visions of sweet-as-sugarplum fairies danced through his head.

As much as he'd denied the break-up being about Troy, and as guilty as he now felt, Michael went to his first gay coffee post-David hoping against hope that Troy would be there.

A good crowd was already gather, but there was no Troy, and luckily no David. Michael got his coffee and joined a few lesbian friends at one of the tables. They were joking and laughing away when who should walk in but Cory, who got his coffee and sat down next to Michael.

"Hey man, heard about you and David. Too bad, you guys were a good couple."

"It's ok. Too bad about you and Troy," Michael lied.

"Things just didn't work out."

"Same with us."

"Well, here's to the next one working," Cory said, lifting his mug.

Michael clicked it with his own. "Cheers man."

Michael and Cory and the rest of the table were still deep in conversation. Michael was having a surprisingly good time, barely even thinking about how his beautiful pilot God wasn't there."

"...so I barely made it to class at all..." David's voice, in mid-story, came through the door. Michael made a point of not looking up, not making eye contact.

"What the fuck!" Cory exclaimed, visibly tensing up next to Michael.

Michael looked at Cory, following his gaze to where David and Troy were ordering their coffees.

Coincidence, Michael thought, it has to be coincidence.

But as they walked by, Michael was sure David was wearing a smug smirk. And as they sat down at a table in the far corner, just the two of them, even Michael had trouble swallowing coincidence as a theory.

"Want to go to 'Stangs and get shit-faced?" Cory asked.

"You know, I really think I do," Michael said. "I really think I do."

Without a look back at their exes, Michael and Cory said their goodbyes and headed over to Mustangs, the college bar where everyone hung out after gay coffee, and they immediately ordered a couple shots of tequila. Each.

"You don't think..." Michael began just as Cory asked, "Are they?" They both chuckled. "Well whatever, " Michael said. "Cheers man." One tequila. Two tequila.

Three tequila.

Four.

Five.

Six.

"Fuck I love this song," Cory said. "I'm gonna go dance. Wanna come?"

"I'm good. I'll watch the table. Sherry and Evan should be here soon anyway."

"K man, back in two shakes."

Michael was definitely feeling the tequila. David and Troy. Really. Where did that... how did they... wow, Cory's actually a good dancer. Really good. Fucking David! How could he? We just broke up. He never even said he liked Troy. Maybe they're just friends. Cory's hot when he dances. Fucking hot. Fuck Troy, fuck David. I'm gonna have fun.

Michael tossed back Tequila Seven and went to dance.

"Cheers," Cory smiled as Michael joined him. "Told you it's a great song."

"Fuckin' rights buddy. Who knew Wonderwall and Closer would mix so well? Let's party."

Within an hour, 'Stangs had its little homo corner as it did every Thursday. Sherry and Evan, the token straight couple of the group, confirmed to Michael after extended hounding that Troy and David had indeed started dating.

Twelve.

Thirteen.

Michael felt the world move as he got up from the table, and he definitely felt himself stumble as he went over to where Cory was chatting up the DJ.

"So I guess our exes are an item."

"Really, man? How you know?"

"David told Sherry tonight at coffee. Well, I guess technically Sherry asked, but only after she caught them in a little liplock in the corner."

"Well good for them," Cory said. "Tequila?"

Michael grinned. "You know, I have something better in mind."

"What?"

"Come with me." Michael grabbed Cory by the wrist, led him through the crowded bar and out the exit.

"Where we going?"

"You'll see," Michael winked. Michael led Cory down the alley beside the bar, till they were far enough in that they weren't visible from the street.

"What..." Corey began. Michael pinned him against the wall and kissed him. Cory tensed and started to pull away but as Michael's hand fumbled with his zipper, Cory relaxed. Michael pulled out Cory's cock and began to stroke it to hardness and when it was fully erect, he dropped to his knees and swallowed it up.

"We really shouldn't be..." Cory began.

Michael looked up. "Want me to stop?"

"Don't you dare," Cory said, putting his hands on Michael's head and guiding him back to work.

When they went back into the bar about ten minutes later, Sherry almost immediately asked "Where have you two been?"

"Just outside talking," Cory said, red-faced.

"Yah, I had to get something off my chest," Michael said, equally red-faced.

"OK, well, Michael, there's a little something you might wanna get off your chin too." She laughed as she walked away.

Michael hurriedly wiped his chin as Cory laughed. "Busted, I guess," he said.

"Who cares?" Michael said. "Tequila?"

"Sounds like a plan. Oh, and Michael?"

"Yes?"

"Thanks, that was good."

Michael blushed. "You know man, anytime."

Cory laughed again. "OK man, what are you doing after the bar?" He grinned and went to dance.

Fuck David. Fuck Troy. I'm single, I'm cute, and I'm gonna fuckin' live it up, Michael thought, as he followed Cory to the dancefloor.

At the Princess Bar, nothing was sacred, nothing stayed secret. It was never intentionally malicious, but sometimes, a scandal was just too juicy to resist spreading. Everyone was equally guilty, and everyone knew starting a conversation with "This is just between us" was a guaranteed way of having that story make the rounds between one happy hour and the next.

Especially if the person you told was Michael or George.

Michael rationalized his gossip by saying that his life was an open book, and that if people did things they were ashamed of, they shouldn't talk about them (they shouldn't have even done them in the first place).

George didn't rationalize his gossip. He just said what he wanted, damn the consequences.

"So I heard Matt fucked Adam this weekend," George told Michael.

It was just the two of them and LBP in the bar, a few days after Jonny had expressed his growing dissatisfaction with Matt. George's unexpected revelation sent Michael reeling. Had Jonny dumped Matt? Had Matt cheated? Were they over? If they were, what did that mean for Michael?

"Where did you hear that?" LBP asked.

"I have my sources." George smiled knowingly.

"Really," Michael said flatly. "Does Jonny know?" Even as Michael asked, his hand was text-messaging Jonny.

-did something happen with you and Matt-

"I dunno if Jonny knows, and don't you say anything. This is between us!"

"Like I would," Michael said.

"Ha!" LBP laughed. "You're the biggest gossip in the city. Telefax, telephone, tell-a-fag."

-why u ask?-

-just curious after what you said the other day-

"Hardly, Little Buddy, have you looked in a mirror lately?"

"Every day, and fuck I'm gorgeous!"

"Round of sambuca!" George yelled. "Let's get this party going."

"Oh fuck," Michael said as the door opened. "Here comes trouble."

Matt walked into the bar as Michael poured him his usual.

-I haven't said anything. Dont say anything either-

-I wont. U coming 2day?-

"And one for Matt," George added, as Michael poured the shots.

"Is Adam coming down tonight?" LBP asked, all fake innocence.

"How would I know?" Matt said.

"I was just asking. Not to anyone specific."

-yah. On my way actually. Matt there yet?-

-just got here. C u in a bit-

"Who are you texting?" George barked.

"Just seein' if Darcy's coming down today."

"Is he?"

"Hasn't decided yet." Quickly Michael texted Darcy. -u comin down?-

-be there in 5- from Jonny

"Was that him?" George asked.

Fuck, Michael thought, lifting his sambuca. "Well let's do these. No point in letting them get cold."

"Here's to men with huge cocks," George toasted.

-be there right away-from Darcy.

-bring treats, one of those days- Michael replied, as the door opened and in walked Adam.

"Oh, Adam!" George said. "Here, sit between me and Matt, you can be the rose between two thorns."

Michael shook his head as he cracked Adam's Kokanee and cleaned away the empty shot glasses.

-oh really? Cant wait to hear-

Michael ran his hand through his hair. One of those days indeed.

Darcy got there just before Jonny, who arrived just as Princess Sophia Maria, Statler, Nelly-belle and Muffin got there.

As he poured their drinks, Michael thought, not for the first time, do we call anyone by their real names anymore?

When everyone was adequately cocktailed, and George had brought the traditional round of sambuca, Michael met Darcy's eyes, and they met as per usual in stall two of the ladies room, away from the prying eye and ears of the bar.

"So..." Darcy prompted as he racked the lines.

"Well, this is between us, but George said Adam and Matt fucked."

"Really. When? Here, you go first."

"This weekend, I guess." Big long sniff. "I don't think Jonny knows. Your go."

"Well, is it even true?" Darcy asked as they switched spots. Big long sniff. "Mmm! I mean, this *is* George we're talking about."

"True. Dunno. I got the impression that things weren't all sunshine, lollipops, and rainbows though."

"Oh? Me good?"

"Yah. Me? Yah, from Jonny."

"Well, we'll see I guess. See you out there."

"Yah thanks, I need that."

Michael took a leak. As he was peeing, his cell vibrated in his pocket. -wazzup with George and Adam-from Jonny

Fuck, Michael thought. As he finished and washed his hands, he replied -whatcha mean- Michael made a point of not looking at Jonny as he came out and rejoined the bar.

-makin all these cracks about Adam and Matt-

-no clue, just being a shit disturber as usual prob-

"Now who is that?" George asked, seeing Michael texting up a storm.

"Just this guy I met at Divas on the weekend."

"Ooh!" LBP clapped his hands. "I smell dirt. Spill!"

"Nothing to spill. Just some random hotty. He's from Vancouver so nothing's gonna happen. Plus he's got that West Coast attitude."

"I hate West Coast guys," Adam said.

"Plenty of hot guys right next to you, hey?" George said with an implying sneer.

"Yah sure," Adam said.

A few rounds of sambucas passed and then Michael again met Darcy's eyes. As they walked towards the bathroom, Darcy asked "So what do you think?"

"I dunno. They seem a little nervous."

Darcy chuckled. "You sure you don't want it to be true just so you can get a crack at Matt?"

"Ha ha ha, very funny. Besides," Michael said as he pushed open the bathroom door, "if Matt and Adam fucked..."

Jonny paused, his eyes widening and the color draining from his face as he walked out of the washroom. "What?"

"Nice move, Michael," Darcy laughed as Jonny stormed to the bar.

By the time Michael and Darcy left the bathroom, they could hear Matt and Jonny yelling from the parking lot.

"Uhm, Michael," George said, "I told you not to say anything."

"It's not my fault."

"For you information, Mikey," Adam snapped, "nothing even happened between me and Matt, he just drove me home."

"It's not my fault."

Jonny stormed back in. "Thanks for telling me, Michael. Adam, you're a fucking whore."

"Wait, I thought you said nothing happened," LBP asked, hanging on very word of the unfolding drama.

"Matt told you?" Adam exclaimed, getting to his feet.

"No, you just did, you idiot," Matt barked, coming in from outside.

"So it's true?" Jonny yelled, storming past Matt and out of the bar.

"Jonny, wait..." Matt yelled as he followed. "Thanks a lot, Michael!" he yelled as he left.

"It's not my fault!"

"Uhm, round of sambuca!"

Whether it was unwanted rebound from David, unresolved feelings for Troy, or unexpected attraction to Cory, Michael fell fast and hard.

That first night, Michael and Cory fucked like the proverbial rabbits, and Michael woke up to Cory straddling him, ready to go again. When Cory rolled off of him, after, and Michael was wiping off his chest, he looked over at Cory lying there, tanned, toned, tattooed, smooth, silky, soft, with a deliciously round butt, he couldn't help but blurt out, "how did I never notice how fucking hot you were?"

"I was always with Troy, you were always with David. Maybe you just didn't notice anyone else."

I sure noticed Troy though, Michael thought. "I'm glad I noticed now." He smiled, and leaned over to kiss Cory. "I had a great time."

"Me too. It was fun."

"What are you up to tonight?"

"Dinner with the family," Cory said with a groan.

"Ha ha, there's advantages to leaving home for school."

"True that."

"Tomorrow?"

"Tomorrow," Cory said with his sly playful smile, "tomorrow, I get to fuck you." He winked.

Michael laughed. "You got it, studmaster." He leaned in and kissed Cory again.

As he walked home from Cory's, Michael felt himself flying. Cory! Troy who? David who? They were already a world away. It was a new day. The dawn of Studmaster. Michael pictured Cory dancing, all by himself on the dancefloor at 'Stangs. What a beautiful body! Such rhythm! Such passion! What a stunning tribal tattoo leading down this incredible ass!

Studmaster!

That weekend was a whirlwind. Cory and Michael barely left the bedroom. They led in bed watching TV. Fucked. Ordered in Chinese. Fucked. Talked. Fucked.

Fucked.

Sunday evening, as they showered off their latest romp, Cory said," I think you should maybe sleep at your place, Michael, I work early tomorrow and don't you have early classes?"

As disappointed as he was, Michael had to admit Cory made

sense. "Well, what about tomorrow?"

"I'll give you a call but it's shaping up to be a crazy work week." He giggled. "For some reason, I didn't get anything done this weekend." He winked that sly playful wink.

"Whyever not?" Michael smiled, leaning in for a kiss as the water ran down over them.

"You've reached Cory. I'm very popular so I'm not here. Talk to me at the beep. BEEP!"

"Hey Cory, it's Michael. Feels like it's been 3 weeks not 3 days huh? Anyway, just seein' if you're going to coffee tomorrow. And 'Stangs after. Maybe we can hook up in the alley again, haha. Old times sakes, you know. Anyway, give me a call when you get in, or I'll see you at coffee tomorrow. K, well, bye for now Studmaster."

In anticipation of seeing Cory at coffee, Michael slept. Barely focused in class. Barely ate. He just pictured Cory, lying there naked, or spilling chow mein down his chest, or dancing up a storm at 'Stangs.

Studmaster.

Michael was the first one in the backroom for Gay Coffee. As he sipped his coffee, he couldn't believe that less than two years ago, he'd been so nervous about setting foot in the door. Robert had moved to Calgary just after Michael and David started dating, but Michael recalled the last thing Robert had said to him.

"You're a great guy, Michael," he'd said in that special mentoring way he always had. "One day, you're going to meet a guy as great as you and all your fairy tales will come true."

As he sat there, two years later, waiting for his Studmaster, Michael knew Robert had been right.

People slowly began to trickle in, but no Cory. Yet. Even as he chatted with his friends, his eyes kept darting to the door, eagerly expecting that smile, that laugh, that Studmaster butt.

David and Troy arrived, luckily sitting as far as possible from Michael. He didn't know if they knew about him and Cory, and he didn't care. Let them sit there making googly eyes at each other. Michael knew they were both just rebounding.

Oh if only Cory would... Yes! There he was! Michael half-rose, then thought better about it and sat down. No point in coming off as too eager. Cory got his coffee and sat down across from Michael.

"Hey," Michael said, with a big goofy grin and a flushing face.

"Hey. Sorry I haven't called, it's been crazy nuts at work."

"You said it might be. Wasn't worried. How's your week been?"

"Long but got great news today!"

"Oh what?"

"Remember my friend Scott I told you about? The one that moved to Vancouver?"

"OK." No, not really.

"He's in town for the weekend. His Greyhound gets in from Calgary at 10. He's meeting us at 'Stangs."

The momentary wave of jealousy faded away at the 'us'. "Cool, can't wait to meet him."

"Yah he's great. Didja hear that, Sher?" he called out to Sherry, who was sitting with Evan and David and Troy. "Scott's in town this weekend."

Sherry shrieked. "I love Scott! He's a dreamboat!"

Who even uses words like dreamboat? Michael thought sullenly. How hot can this guy, this Scott, really be?

Michael only had to wait a couple hours to find out.

"That guy's gay?" Michael asked Sherry.

"You'd never have thought so, hey? All the good ones are."

"Hey!" Evan said, "I heard that!"

"All the good ones but you babe, let's dance." Sherry and Evan left Michael sitting there alone, as he watched Cory and Scott do shots at the bar.

They're just friends, Michael told himself. So what if they're having a little reunion? At the end of the night, it'll be me and my Studmaster.

Cory and Scott came back to the table. "Oh sorry man, I should've got you one."

"No worries, I'll go get one," Michael said. "And some shots for us too." He grinned. Scott might be Hot Vancouver Muscle Man but at the end of the night, he'll be sleeping alone.

The next three hours were a blur. Showing how non-jealous he was, Michael bought shots after shots even as he listened to the endless parade of "Hey remember when..." and "oh my god that time when we..." Apparently Cory and Scott, buddies since third grade, had grown up together, came out together, gone to University together... in fact, it was almost surprising that Cory hadn't moved to Vancouver with Scott back in '94.

"I had just got my job," Cory said by way of explanation.

"And I was in love with whats-his-face? With the ties?"

"Alex!"

"Yah Alex! What a tool he turned out to be," Scott laughed. "But I followed him to Vancouver, and well, three years later, no Alex, and here I am."

"But it's just the weekend right?"

"Fuckin rights. Vancouver man. Davie Street. There's more queers in the Odyssey on a Saturday night than in this whole city. And that's just one bar. Deathbridge can't hold a candle to it."

"So why are you back?" Michael asked.

"It's my little sis' wedding on Saturday. Figured I'd get in early to party with Tatty here since we won't be able to party much at the wedding."

"Beg pardon?"

"Didn't he tell you? He's my date for the wedding, and lemme tell you, from how my parents were when I came out, to think they'd let me bring a guy..."

"When were you planning on telling me?" Michael yelled at Cory.

"What's the big deal? We didn't have plans."

"Because you didn't call me all week."

"Calm down, dude."

"Wait a minute," Scott said. "Are you guys together?"

Before Michael could reply, Cory said, "no, we're just friends. I don't know what..."

"Well what was all last weekend then?"

"Michael, calm down."

"Well, let me ask 'Beefy' then. Me and 'Tatty' had sex for like four days straight! Does that sound like just friends?" Michael was screaming, oblivious to the stares he was getting.

"It was fun but it was just sex, Michael. I thought you knew that."

"Well I didn't! I thought we shared something! I thought we really connected!"

"Maybe I should..." Scott said, starting to get up. Even with the dance music thumping, more and more faces were watching the unfolding drama.

"No no," Cory said, pulling Scott back into his chair. "Michael, go home, I'll call you Monday."

"Are you two fucking?"

"That's none of your..."

"Are you?"

"Yes alright? Are you fucking happy?" Cory shouted back. "That's what we do whenever we're together. I don't know what you thought was happening but grow the fuck up."

Tears stung Michael's eyes. "Go to hell, Cory."

"Catch a fucking cab, Michael. You're a fucking mess."

"I'll walk, asshole."

"Dude, don't be retarded. You live on the fucking west side."

"I know where I live, thanks." Michael slammed his beer down on the table. Foam sprayed everywhere. He stormed away, the tears welling up, flowing. He didn't care who saw. Just as he reached the exit, Scott grabbed his arm.

"What the fuck do you want?"

"Take a cab man. That's a long walk. It's cold out."

"Shouldn't you be fucking my boyfriend and ruining my life? I'll walk."

"Suit yourself." Scott turned to go back to the table.

"Before you got here everything was fine!"

Scott looked Michael in the eye. "Dude, before I got here, nothing was different."

"Fuck you! You don't know!" Michael stormed out of the bar, stumbling through the people at the exit, ignoring the grunts, the swears, the 'faggot' as he pushed his way through.

He could barely see through the tears as he stormed away from Mustangs. Away from Cory. Away from Mr. Vancouver-is-so-great-why-don't-I-go-back-home-and-ruin-peoples-lives.

The wind whipped him; he didn't care.

The tears burned on his fiery face; he didn't care.

The bridge stretched out in front of him, Whoop-up Drive crossing the Old Man; he felt a brief pang of fear at the thought of walking it but shook it off, tears and snot flying from his face. He was so mad, soooo mad! How could Cory have done that? "What a fucking asshole!" he screamed out, half expecting it to echo off the coulees.

"What An Asshole!" he roared, and began to run across the bridge, up, up, up the hill, just wanting to get home.

That's when the inevitable happened. He tripped, fell to the ground, just as a car pulled up beside him. The window rolled down. It was David.

"Oh fucking great."

"Get in, dummy. I'll give you a ride."

"No! I can walk." He went to get up, fell back down, started puking.

"Oh God," David sighed. He got out of the car, came around. "Let me drive you home please," he said.

"Get away from me! I don't want you to see me like this."

"I've seen you puke, babe!" David chuckled.

"Don't fucking laugh at me!"

David grabbed Michael by the arms. "I am driving you home. Calm down now."

Michael sniffed back more tears, wiped the spittle from his lips with the back of a bloody hand. He looked up into David's face... into his sweet brown puppy dog eyes. "OK."

In the car, Michael wouldn't look at David at all.

"I am such an idiot. Such an idiot."

"Wanna tell me what happened?"

Michael sniffed. "Where's Troy?" he asked in that snotty sneery way David hated.

"Is that what this is about?"

"No!"

"OK good. He's at home. I have an exam tomorrow."

"Oh."

"Wanna tell me what happened?"

"I'd rather not. Just drunk and stupid."

"We've all been there."

"Not you."

"Well, not me, true, but I'm practically perfect in every way." David smiled. "Well, here we are."

"Did you... well, did you wanna come up?"

"Michael..."

"No, no, not like that. I just thought I might need a hand up the stairs." He giggled nervously.

"Is Genie home?"

"She's at her boyfriends."

David sighed. "OK. Fuck, you're high maintenance."

"I love you too."

"Michael..."

Michael laughed, still sniffing. "Sorry sorry, my bad."

David parked, then helped Michael upstairs, Michael wobbling, stumbling. "Christ, how did you get so far on your own?"

"Sheer drunken luck."

"Damn right. Wanna tell me what happened?"

"No."

"Well, here we are."

"Sure you won't come in?"

"I think you can make it to your bed on your own."

Michael looked into those sweet melting-caramel puppy-dog eyes. "Maybe I don't want to be in bed on my own."

"Michael..."

"Sorry sorry... kind of."

"You broke up with me."

"Doesn't tonight prove I'm an idiot?"

"Michael..." less plaintively.

"Doesn't everyone get a second chance?"

"Michael..." even less plaintively. And closer.

"'I'll bottom."

Forty-five minutes later, as Michael dozed off in David's arms, he whispered, half-asleep, "I love you."

Equally half-asleep, David whispered back. "I love you too... don't tell Troy."

Michael was softly snoring.

-Jonny! Call me or text me or somethin. I'm sorry man-

-Matt dont be pissed. I didn't know, it was an accident-

-Adam, honestly, I didn't mean anything. Txt me back stud-

-Darcy, please say you have treats and are on your way-

-LBP, it's eviction night. Live! Bring blizzards! Yaaay Julie-

"If you're done texting!" George yelled.

"What? Oh sorry. Sambuca?"

"No, not yet. We need to talk."

Never good, Michael thought as he sat down on the counter behind the Princess Bar.

"Well, I wanted you to hear it from me."

Ominously not good, Michael thought.

"Waldorf had a stroke last night."

Michael stared off into space even as his phone began to vibrate. "Is he ok?"

"We don't know. Statler said he'd call when he knew. People will ask though."

"Well yah he hasn't missed a day since what? 2004? When he had pneumonia?"

"That was '03. '04 is when his mother died."

"Oh right," Michael said blankly as his phone vibrated again.

"Well, he's not dead so the bar goes on."

"Of course," he said, equally blankly. "Is Statler coming in tonight?" His phone vibrated again.

"Have you ever seen one without the other?"

"Of course not," he said, running his hand through his hair. "George, what if..."

"No what ifs! Old people die! Now quick, before all those other princesses get here, two sambuca, you and me!"

"Yah of course," Michael said as he blankly poured two shots. The vibration started again.

Statler and Waldorf had been coming to Choices for forty years.

They had been best friends and roommates before that, for another fifteen years or so, back when the only gay places in Edmonton were hotel pubs. How people knew which ones, Michael had never gotten around to asking. Like so many other questions.

They weren't dead yet, Michael reminded himself.

-I'm fine. Later-from Jonny.

-Whatever-from Matt.

-Not your fault. I guess. See you tomorrow-from Adam.

-I need a night off, honey. See you on the weekend-from Darcy.

Damn! thought Michael as it vibrated again.

-They better evict that fucking rat! Oreo right?-from LBP.

Michael replied as George and Princess Sophia talked about the upcoming Bear-Leather-Denim-Cowboy Two Hundred 1/2 Men Extravaganza.

Statler and Waldorf weren't their real names of course; hardly anyone went by real names at the Princess Bar. Although technically they weren't princesses. Just regulars. Not in George's chosen circle, for sure.

Dennis and Bruce were only called Statler and Waldorf because they sat there at the bar, heads together, negatively commenting on everything from drink prices to shows to what was on TV to how loud the music was to the fact that it was harder to pick up dates at 73 than at 37 (or 45, or 52, or 61).

Neither Statler nor Waldorf had had a trick from Choices since Michael had been around.

Their whole life was each other.

If Waldorf... when Waldorf... when one of them died, what would happen?

So many questions.

"It's weird without all the chicken here," Princess Sophia said.

"Blame that on Michael," George said.

"It's not my fault."

"What did you do, Michael?"

"Nothing. George told me that Adam and Matt fucked. It's his fault."

"Adam and Matt what?"

"Oh fuck. How did you know anyway George?"

"A little birdie told me," George said with a smug smile.

-Whatcha doin after work-from Jonny.

"Who's that?"

"No one!"

"Another home for you to wreck?" Princess Sophia asked.

"No!"

They both laughed as Michael texted Jonny back. -why wazzup-

"Sambucas!" George yelled with a smile.

Statler and Waldorf drove Michael crazy. That's why he'd nicknamed them after the two cranky old men on the Muppets. Their endless complaining about everything! They even carried earplugs in case the music got too loud!

If you come down tonight guys, Michael thought, I'll keep the music real low.

-I wanna get drunk. Meet me at Divas when ur off-

-ok Jonny, c u at 12-

The phone rang. The real phone. Not a cell phone.

"Choices!" Michael said. "Uh huh, uh huh, uh huh, thanks for calling and telling us." He hung up.

"Who was that?"

"Statler. Waldorf's gonna be OK. He's staying in the hospital 'til Thursday but they should be here for the weekend.

"Good," George said. "Tell the DJ to crank it."

Statler and Waldorf didn't quite make George's list of princesses to party with.

After an eight-hour shift at Choices, Divas was always a bit of culture shock.

And, used to seeing Jonny mostly sober in the happy hours of early evening, seeing him smashed at midnight was even more culture shock.

"Awobudsup."

"What?"

"Hello bud. Whats up? I'm drunk."

"Yah you are."

"Shots!"

"Do you really need more?"

"Did your boyfriend cheat on you?"

"Not recently," Michael admitted. "Shots!"

After some shots and completely ignoring the amateur strip contest going on on stage, Michael asked Jonny "Why are you so upset if you weren't happy?"

"I had doubts. Just doubts. I didn't go out and stick my cock in some other guy."

"Point." Michael tried to lighten the subject by adding, "I always figure you were the top not Matt."

"Well I am. But he put his cock where it didn't shouldn't have gone, and I'll tell you this," he said, progressively slurring, "I never let Matt put his cock in my in me but I'd let you do it if you want to do it." He slid partially out of the chair and into Michael's arms. "You want to take me fuck and home me?" He hiccoughed. "Take me fuck and home me I mean?" He looked at Michael with bleary but beautiful eyes. Michael didn't have the heart to tell him he was repeating his gibberish.

"I'll take you home at least."

"Nope! Not goin' home. Imma sleep at your place."

"Well ok but just sleep."

"Well ok then we'll just sleep in the bed that had the guy that put his cock in..." He hiccoughed. "Yah."

"Let me get you to bed."

"That's what I been sayin!" Jonny said, getting up and promptly falling down.

"Here, let me help you," Michael picked Jonny up, his arms around his (hard pecs) chest as Jonny draped his (bulging bicep) arm over Michael's shoulder.

As Michael helped Jonny through the crowd and down the stairs to street level, all he could think was that it was very good that noone from the PBC really ever frequented Divas.

Luckily, Michael only lived a block and a half away from Divas, so the stumbling distance was short. He got Jonny into the building, into the elevator, out of the elevator, into the apartment, out of his shoes, into the bedroom, and with one final drop, into his bed.

He was lying there, muscle shirt, boarder shorts, eyes closed, hands limp at his side. Strangely attractive. For a drunken mess.

Michael smiled and started to pull a cover over top of him. Jonny grabbed his wrist. "Get inna bed. Imma gonna ride you all night..." His sentence broke off and shortly, he began to snore.

Michael smiled again, looking down on him. He really is really pretty, he thought, pulling the covers over the biceps, pecs, and (huge!) bulge.

Michael lay down on top of the covers on the other side of the bed. He lay there in the darkness, listening to Jonny snore as Jonny rolled onto his side, as the moon came in through the window, bathing Jonny in a subtle warm glow.

Michael too turned on his side. A cuddle can't hurt right? He thought. He shuffled closer to Jonny, slowly, softly, lad his arm across Jonny's chest and snuggled in closer 'til they were spooning. Jonny continued to snore even as Michael's hand softly stroked Jonny's chest and abs through his shirt.

Jonny stopped snoring, took Michael's hand and guided it down to the (huger!) bulge. He put Michael's hand firmly on the firmness, and, pulling Michael closer with his right arm, he whispered, "don't tell Matt."

When Michael woke up the next morning, Jonny was gone.

When Michael woke up the next morning, David was gone, and Michael's head hurt.

How the fuck did I get home? he thought.

Even thinking hurt.

Why aren't I at Cory's? Oh yah. There was something about some Scott... oh for fuck sake! What an ASS I made of myself. I can't fucking believe I walked fucking home. Jesus H Christ. Fuck.

Wincing from the hangover, he got into his housecoat and went out for coffee.

"And how are we today?" his roommate asked. Genie's (needlessly) civil tone was like nails on a chalkboard, except the chalkboard was his eyeballs.

"Grrr ugh argh."

"So I thought you and David were over? I mean, I thought you were all gung ho about this Cory guy."

"I am. We are. Why would you..." Michael went white. "Oh. Fuck. Me."

Genie laughed. "That's what I heard all last night."

"Weren't you at your boyfriends?"

"We slept here. Aren't you cheating on your new boyfriend with your ex-boyfriend?"

"Oh. Fuck. Me."

"I could..." Genie laughed, "but I really think you have your hands full without suddenly deciding you're a bisexual bottom wanting to be topped by his oh-so-sexy female roommate." She giggled again.

"Oh. Fuck. Me."

"You've reached Michael and Genie! We both have light brown hair so tell us which one you want. After the beep. BEEP!"

"Michael, it's Cory. I'll call you Monday. Leave me alone this weekend."

"Michael, it's David. Last night was great, but you were drunk and I was stupid. Don't tell Troy!"

"Michael, it's Troy! What the fuck did you do? How could you? I was just using David to get to you but then you fell in love with my ex and then slept with your ex, my boyfriend... haha sorry hun, just can't. It's Jamie dude, Genie and I are just fucking with you. Peace out."

What a fucking cunt, Michael thought.

When Michael rolled over and opened his eyes, and didn't see Jonny, he was relieved. Oh, his sore butt and the condom wrapper on the headboard told him what had happened as surely as they told him that Jonny hadn't bent over like promised. He hadn't been that drunk. Drunk at all really. But still, he'd hoped it had been a dream (a fucking hot dream where he got pounded for an hour before they both finally shot their loads). But a dream nonetheless.

But in the morning (well, in the afternoon), Jonny was gone, Michael was alone, and goddam - thank God noone at Choices knew anything.

So when Michael got to work, and George said nothing, and LBP and Darcy and Nelly Belle came for their drinks, Michael knew he was in the clear.

Darcy being on a blow break, Michael treated himself in the bathroom about an hour into a very happy hour. As he was on his way out of the washroom, Matt was on his way into the bar.

BAM!

Matt slapped Michael across the face.

"What the..." All Michael could see was spots.

"First," Matt yelled, slapping Michael again. "First, you tell him that I fucked up and did Adam without even knowing it was true, much less why it happened. Then," he continued, "then you get him so shitfaced that you get him into bed and completely take advantage of him."

"What the..."

"Don't even deny it!" As Matt's hand flew for a third time, Michael grabbed it. "Jonny told me everything! If you ever stood a chance with me, you have totally blown it. You're nothing but a gossipy, slutty, manipulative, loser bartender with a drug habit and a small dick." The other hand came up and slapped Michael across the face.

Matt stormed out.

Michael stood there, head spinning, from the slaps, the drugs.

"Uhm, if you're done your little domestic quarrel," George began, "round of sambuca."

What a fucking cunt, Michael thought, casually wiping off any VCR as he held his smarting cheeks.

The Princess Bar was very forgiving of scandal. They had forgiven Drag Empress IX for ignoring Choices her whole reign. They had forgiven former co-owner Jim for being a murderer (even if the province hadn't). They had forgiven Darcy, many moons ago as a Choices bartender, for stealing money from the AIDS jar for drugs. Hell, they forgave George almost daily for the racist, sexist, homophobic, HIVaphobic, politically-incorrect evil slander that typically spewed forth from his mouth.

They'd forgiven many a homewrecker, and many a homewreckee.

They forgave.

But they never forgot.

They 'forgot' things like drugs, like drunk driving, like drinking at other bars. It was easy to forget things you ignored.

There were lots of things too that they never forgave. For customers in the bar in general (commoners as they were called), violence, tragic drunkenness, trashy promiscuity, et cetera, they never forgave, never forgot.

In their own little circle? Well, it took a lot to be no longer welcomed at the Princess Bar. When it did happen, it was clear.

Even if you managed to snag a stool, the rounds of sambuca, George-bought or not, skipped you.

You were greeted, then ignored.

When you walked in, you didn't get "Oh fuck" from the bartender.

You got "what can I get for you sir?"

These were the subtle signs of excommunication. Had Michael not been the bartender, he knew he'd've received such a sign. Not because of what had happened. Divorces, affairs, these things happened all the time.

But never, NEVER, in the fifteen years of the Princess Bar, in the thirty years of Choices, had any simple homewrecking scandal divided the bar.

Until the Matt/Jonny/Michael/Adam love-triangle-with-an-extra-angle happened.

Matt and Jonny both avoided Choices in the days following, wrapped up in the domestic issues of the pending divorce. Some blamed Matt. Some blamed Jonny. Many blamed Michael. Few blamed Adam.

And then a text was sent that stirred it all up again, only a few days after the Jonny/Michael scandal broke.

-why would you have said anything? Ur hot, and I really wanted you to fuck me but now I dunno-

Sent to Michael.

By Adam.

Intercepted by LBP while Michael was in the bathroom (stall 2).

When Michael came out, LBP handed him his phone. "You have a new text."

"oh?"

"It's Adam, wanting a fuck."

As Michael stood there, floored, the real phone rang.

"Choices! Uh huh. Uh huh. Uh huh. Uh huh. I'll tell them. Uh huh. Thanks for calling." Michael hung up the phone. "Waldorf's dead."

The PBC was silent, then George said softly," round of sambuca please, and pour one for Bruce."

"Bruce Michael Thompson, 1932-2009. Uncle and Friend. Went to sleep knowing he was survived by a family that loved him. In lieu of flowers..."

"Whatever!" George said.

"Are we having a memorial?" Michael asked, putting down the obit from the paper.

"No."

"But..."

"But what?"

"He's been here since Day One."

"Michael, you're still a kid. I'm a lot older. We've done this. For fifteen years, all I did was go to memorials at bars. For friends." He paused. "Bars are for the living. Waldorf's dead."

"That's harsh."

"That's life! You're a kid, and all you care about is your faggy little dramas. We get it. You don't."

"That's not fair, George. I understand."

"How many funerals have you gone to?"

"Why does that..."

"How many?"

"Like three."

"Go to three a month. For twelve years. We don't care if you fucked Jonny or Jonny fucked you or Matt fucked Adam or Adam fucked the whole bar. You need to understand that. It's time to face the real world, Michael, people die all the time. Grow the fuck up!"

"Sambuca?"

"That's the princess I trained! Sambuca!"

"So did you hear Cory's moving to Vancouver?" Sherry asked Michael.

"Cory's what to where with who and why?"

"Cory... is moving... to Vancouver... with Hotty McScotty."

"When?"

"This week I guess."

"Really."

"You sound upset."

"Nope. Not at all."

"Oh my God! You and Cory really did..."

"Doesn't matter."

"I am so sorry Michael. I always thought you had a thing for Troy. And I figured, Cory moving, Troy single, you'd be happy."

"What?"

"You'd be happy."

"Before that."

"Troy single?"

"Yah."

"Since when?"

"Since this morning apparently when David dumped him."

"David dumped him? But David told me not to tell..."

"Busted!"

"What?"

"I bluffed you. Troy said he's single but didn't say why. Thanks Michael."

"What about David?"

"He's not answering his phone. Maybe he will for you."

"Why would I call?"

"Don't you wanna get back together?"

Cory moving... Troy single... "Where would you get that idea?"

"Aren't you still in love with David?"

"Why would..."

"Didn't you say so last night?"

"Maybe, I dunno, but Sherry... it's Troy. He's like the man of my dreams."

There was an odd click. "Hey Michael, it's David. You're off speaker phone now but thanks. That was all I needed to know."

The silence that followed was deep. Michael stared at the silent receiver. What the hell did he just do?

It didn't make sense.

There wasn't a logical connection.

Just days before, no one was talking to anyone else. They didn't even want to be in the same room.

Now they were all here.

Same place, same time.

"For every day, pretty much, of the last ten years, pretty much at 7:17, Waldorf would walk in and order his Scotch on the rocks. At about 7:41, he'd order his second. When happy hour ended, he'd get a large jug of beer, which lasted him, pint by pint, until 9:37 when he would leave to catch the bus home."

Michael stood behind the bar, talking on the cordless microphone, to the current PBC and the PBC of years before, come to say goodbye. George's wishes or not, the impromptu memorial had just materialized.

"He was a bastard," Michael continued. "Bruce you bastard, we would say. Got that right, he would reply. Before he left the bar, every single night since I've been working, he would bang his fists on the bar and ask why the music had to be so goddam loud. At which point he would pull out his earplugs.

'We're sitting here in a bar that Waldorf... Bruce.. was at forty years ago. Some of us weren't of age. Some of us weren't even born. And he was gay, and sitting here in Edmonton's first gay bar, with his gay friend Statler... Dennis I mean... and I can hear him saying, no, yelling, to turn down the Diana Ross then as much as he yelled to turn down the Lady Gaga now.

'Bruce Michael Thompson... Waldorf..." Michael raised his shot of ouzo, and everyone did likewise. "Wherever you are, I hope the music's not too loud and that the buses are on time.

'Cheers!"

Eighty-some people "Cheers-ed" back.

Eighty-some shots of ouzo.

Even in death, some princesses at the Princess Bar would not drink sambuca.

Only in death did George indulge them.

"Another round of ouzos!" he yelled, and wiping a tear away, Michael happily and obediently obliged.

"I'm really sorry, it's not my fault," Michael said as he filled Matt's shot glass with another ouzo.

Adam was seven seats right, Jonny four seats left. Gotta love the Princess Bar.

"You should have stayed out of it."

"Well, you're talking to me at least."

"It doesn't mean much. It's not the time or the place to get mad."

"Fair."

"I will be mad at you later though. When are you done work?"

"Not till 12."

"That's a long way."

"Exactly. Do you work tomorrow?"

"No. I called in earlier cuz I knew I was gonna get smashed at this memorial."

"Oh."

"K fuck off now, I am done faking nice. Go serve customers that like you."

"Ouch!" Michael said as he walked away. Within seconds, his phone vibrated.

-I think I should get to fuck you too-

-what Matt?-

-well Jonny did-

-Jonny did, YOU THINK!-

-Jonny did though-

-yah-

-Can I fuck you tonight-

-Really-

-Yes really-

-You're fucking with me Matt. That's not kewl. I said I was sorry-

-Get over yourself. Go to the girls can, stall 2-

That's weird, Michael thought. That's the coke spot. Matt doesn't do coke. Does he?

Michael walked into the girls, into stall 2.

There was Matt, sitting on the toilet tank, phone in one hand, hard cock in the other.

"About time," Matt said.

Even as Michael engulfed that hard Matt cock with his mouth, he couldn't help but wonder how much coke powder was on Matt's ass. Not that Matt's ass needed improving. Michael grabbed onto it with both hands as his mouth descended onto the so-so-soooo-hard-uncut-cock in front of him.

If service was slow at the bar, they shouldn't be drinking so fast anyway, Michael thought. Waldorf always drank slow.

The important thing was, as he went down on Matt, that everyone was thinking about Waldorf.

When Michael walked into gay coffee the next Thursday, it was busy and it was angry. He knew everyone was thinking of him, talking about him. Some were talking about how he'd blown up in a drunkenly disgraceful disaster over Cory. Some were talking about how he'd fucked over David again and again. Some were talking about how he was so in love with Troy.

It was never gonna happen, they all agreed.

But Michael wanted it to, they all agreed.

And with Cory moving to Vancouver, and David boycotting anything gay in Lethbridge out of an understandable desire to avoid Michael, there was Troy, and there was Michael.

For gay coffee that Thursday, Troy and Michael outranked any Ross-Rachel drama that NBC could concoct.

For gay coffee in Lethbridge, Must-See-TV happened in one place: the backroom of a coffee shop where no one even had the chance of using "We were on a break" as an excuse.

An hour after gay coffee, when Michael and Troy were watching Friends, from the semi-naked seclusion of Troy's bed, Michael didn't give a fuck who'd broken what with who, who was thinking about whom, and David Cory Kevin who?

It was Michael.

With Troy.

Finally.

And Forever.

It happened so easily. With everything that had happened, with David, with Cory moving, it was a brief fifteen minutes of conversation over cappuccinos, and the casual mentioning of a weekend of wild Studmaster sex, and Troy invited Michael over.

At first, he was almost too nervous to get hard.

This was Troy.

His beautiful pilot God.

...

This was Troy.

His beautiful pilot God.

Nerves faded, and being hard wasn't an issue.

In the post-orgasmic afterglow, Troy said, "don't take this the wrong way but don't read too much into this."

"Hmmm?"

"It was fun, don't get me wrong, but I don't think we should start up anything."

"Oh?"

"With everything that's just happened, it's just too soon. If anything's gonna happen, it's best we give it time. Take things slow."

"Oh... ok... not a big deal."

"Still, it was fun, and Lord knows you're cute. Just don't wanna rush into something big."

"Don't worry, Troy. If something more happens, cool. If not..." Michael shrugged, as his heart crumbled.

"But wanna go to a movie tomorrow anyway?"

"Sure," Michael said, as the crumbling heart began to beat again.

Sex now.

Movie tomorrow.

Michael and Troy.

Finally.

Forever.

Michael remembered the first time he'd seen Matt. It was lust at first sight. Bright green eyes and a dimpled smile, cute butt, mussed brown hair.

And then, of course, Jonny came in, in all his dark-haired, blue-eyed beauty, and the burgeoning Matt fantasy was shot to hell.

Regardless, for two years, Michael lusted after Matt, and what's more, really started to fall for him. Matt was smart. Clever. Passionate about life. Hard-working. Not a flake like so many other gay boys his age. Matt was perfect.

Matt was also with Jonny.

But then BAM!

Matt meets Adam. Matt fucks Adam. Jonny dumps Matt. Jonny fucks Michael. Matt finds out. Michael sucks off Matt in the washroom at Choices during a memorial service for Waldorf.

And as planned, after Michael shut down Choices, instead of going to Divas like he normally would've done, he went over to Matt's. How could he not? This was Matt! The guy he'd been in love with for two years.

Michael swallowed hard as he pressed Matt's buzzer.

"Hey it's me."

"C'mon up."

Matt (and Jonny?) lived on the fifteenth floor of one of the new condos springing up all over downtown. The lobby was gorgeous, the elevator was fast. It made Michael's little bachelor pad in Oliver look pretty dingy by comparison.

Then again, two successful graphic designers fresh out of University likely commanded higher salaries than a bartender. Thank God for tips from successful graphic designers, Michael thought, as he knocked on the door.

The door opened and Michael barely had time to notice Matt standing there only in a towel, before Matt grabbed him by the front of the shirt and pulled him in, down. Door shut. Towel dropped. Clothes torn off. In the frantic frenzied fucking that followed, any guilt Michael felt evaporated.

This was Michael.

And Matt.

Finally.

And Forever.

In the post-orgasmic afterglow, Michael said, "so are you and Jonny done then?"

Matt looked up from where his head lay on Michael's chest. His eyes sparkled and he giggled that giggle he giggled so well. "I don't know but I'm sure not done with you. I just don't know why it's taken so long to have your dick in me."

"You know I've wanted to put it in you since the day we met."

"I know."

"Timing just sucked."

"Speaking of sucked..." Matt said, and the conversation stopped again for a while.

In the next post-orgasmic afterglow, Michael asked, "So where *is* Jonny?"

"He's staying at his mom's while we work things out."

"So can I sleep over?"

"I have to be up and gone at 7 though."

"I thought you called in."

"I lied to get you over."

"I would've come anyway."

"Good."

"So can I sleep over?"

"Yah. And we should sleep now. Seven comes early."

"Ugh. So early."

Matt rolled onto his side, his back to Michael. Michael reached out his hand and traced Matt's spine with his fingertips down to that perfect Matt ass. Had he really just fucked that? Twice? Wow. It was everything he'd imagined. More. As Matt sank back into Michael's arms and began to snore, Michael kissed his cheek.

In the morning, Michael woke up to Matt sucking him off. After he swallowed, Matt rolled over, jerked off, then jumped out of bed, "OK, I gotta go to work. Are you going back to sleep?"

"Is that OK?"

"Sure. I'll be home at lunch."

"Jonny won't be back?"

Matt shrugged the shrug he shrugged so well. "Who cares? It's my condo."

"OK."

"K. See you around 12."

Michael fell back asleep, woke up around 11, and had just showered and gotten dressed when Matt got home. "Why are you wearing clothes?" he said, his hands fast at work on Michael's jeans.

"Don't you need to eat?"

"Mmmhmm," Matt murmured, his mouth full, his hand jerking himself. Michael's hands got tangled in Matt's hair as his hips began to thrust. "Fuck," he said, as speed increased. "I'm gonna cum." Matt pulled off and jerked Michael off onto his face as he let loose another load all over his shirt. "K I gotta change," he said, "then where should we go for lunch?"

They had lunch, then Michael waited anxiously for Matt to finish the day at work. Then they fucked. Then had dinner. Then they fucked. Then they watched a move and cuddled. In the morning, Michael woke to yet another incredible blowjob. Matt went to work. Michael dozed 'til Matt woke him up for lunch. "Call in sick," he said, "let's go to Calgary for the weekend."

"Really?"

"Yah, let's go. We need a change of scene after all the drama."

"What are we gonna do in Calgary?"

"We're going to get a hotel and you're going to spend the night fucking me."

"Let me call in."

"Uh Choices!" George answered the phone.

"It's Michael. I can't leave the bathroom without puking. There's no way I can come in."

"Fucking kids! Who is supposed to cover for you with no notice?"

"I don't know."

"Get your act together! I'm not happy!"

"I'm sorry... oh... I gotta go..." Michael said, making a heaving sound as he hung up.

"I'm off," he grinned.

The car was barely out of the city before Matt's pants were off.

Those first weekends with Troy were a blur. A sweaty naked blur. "Giving things time" fell apart, in candlelit dinners; cramped, comical, yet still sexy bubble baths for two; Troy showing up with flowers only to get flowers from Michael when he opened the door. It was a corny made-for-TV movie, and the two main characters were finally getting their big romantic montage.

Michael went to school. Troy went to work. Troy flew his flights from here to there; Michael flew without moving, flights of fancy in his mind to a future sparkling with weddings-on-a-hot-summer-day, sunset-walks-on-distant-beaches, white-picket-fence fantasies of the life he knew he and Troy were going to have.

"Wanna go to Calgary for the weekend?" Troy asked. "I'm free and we could hit the clubs, get out of the 'Bridge."

A road trip with the man of his dreams? "Sure!"

"K. I'll call Robert, see if we can stay in his guest room. I'll call you back."

Michael hurriedly packed. A weekend away from the familiar faces of 'Stangs, up in the "big city", where he could dance to Spice Girls without feeling awkward, where he could lean over in the bar and kiss Troy anytime he wanted. It would be wonderful.

When Troy picked him up an hour later, he said, "I figured we could use the time to get to know each other a bit better. It's weird, how you can know someone for a year or whatever, and not really know much about them."

Good sign that, Michael thought. "And we've been pretty preoccupied lately."

"True." Troy winked.

It was only a couple hours drive, but it felt even faster to Michael. They talked family, work, coming out, sex (no ex-boyfriends though, no Cory, no David). They talked books and movies and music and daydreams and future plans for their lives. The miles sped by in the summer sun and it wasn't long until they were pulling up outside of Robert's condo just off 17th Ave (aka Gay Central Calgary).

For how close it was to Lethbridge, Michael hadn't been up to Calgary often. Once with David and another time with a carload of friends. Both times, it was a quick drive up Saturday to drink and dance at Metro, then home after Last Call.

A weekend away with the man of his dreams was a new thing entirely.

"In case I forget to mention it," Michael said, "I had a great weekend."

"God, you're corny," Troy said, and leaned over to kiss Michael's cheek. The brush of Troy's perfectly trimmed scruff against Michael's cheek was among the most wonderful sensations Michael had ever experienced. The kiss on the cheek found lips, and with a soft grunt of pleasure, that kiss lengthened until there was a banging on the window.

"If you guys need a room, I have one ready." Robert hollered through the glass. They laughed. "Come on in, guys. Cocktails are poured."

Inside Robert's house, they enjoyed their Cosmos as he gave them the grand tour, being sure to draw attention to the "mints" he'd left on their pillows ("Mint flavored condoms! Isn't that a gas?")

"I just want to shower quick before we go out," Troy said. "I'll be quick."

"It'll give us a chance to catch up," Robert said with a smile.

Troy pecked Michael on the cheek and went off to their room. Robert patted on the cushion next to him on the sofa. "So, how is everything going back in Lethbridge?"

Michael sat down. All the drama that had led up to this didn't seem to matter now. He felt himself grin. "That good hey?" Robert said. "I remember when you first came out, how much of a little crush you had on him. And now, here we are. Was that only a couple years ago? My!"

"It's new, it's exciting."

"Oh, I remember those feelings. When I first met my lover Ron we had six months of that."

"Only six months?"

"Then we moved in together and it was all new and exciting again."

"I don't think you ever mentioned Ron before."

"No, I don't talk about him much."

"Why did you guys break up?"

"Oh, we didn't break up. Ron passed away in '91. We'd been together nearly a decade."

"I'm sorry... I didn't,..."

"Oh it's ok, Michael. I've said my goodbyes long ago, and it doesn't hurt anymore. Just a warm glow where he used to be." There was an uncomfortable silence. "How's your drink?"

"How did he... oh, I could use another."

Robert got up and crossed over to the bar where he began to shake another batch of Cosmos. "It was just pneumonia at the end. Almost a relief in a way. We'd seen so many go through so much worse."

"Just pneumonia?"

"Well, it's a lot more complicated when you're positive."

"Oh..."

"Sorry, Michael, I thought you knew I was positive."

"No."

"Well, I'm in good health otherwise, so no worries there."

"That's good." Robert handed him a drink and chuckled. "You're uncomfortable."

"No, I just... I've never met anyone who's positive before."

"Oh, you have."

"Who?"

"That's for them to tell you. Unless you're going to have sex with them, it doesn't really matter, does it?"

"No, I guess not." They sipped their drinks.

"Just getting dressed guys!" Troy called from down the hall.

"I'm going to go pretty up," Michael said, and, Cosmo in hand, went and joined Troy, who was pulling on his jeans.

As they stood there, both styling their hair, Michael looked at the reflection of them in the mirror and let his mind wander, thirty, forty years down the road. Two old men, wrinkled, liver spots, styling their grey hair in a mirror. Then one reflection faded. Just one sad old man.

"Whatcha thinking about?" Troy asked, his scruff brushing Michael's cheek as he wrapped his arms around his waist from behind. "Your hair's fine."

"Did you know Robert has AIDS?"

"I know he's HIV-positive, yes," Troy emphasized.

"Oh. I didn't. It just threw me I guess."

"Don't let it. We're here to have a fun weekend."

"You're right," Michael said, twisting around in Troy's arms and kissing him. "Let's go dance."

T he night in Calgary was a blur for Michael. He and Matt barely left the hotel. They ordered in. They went for a swim in the hotel pool (where a cleaning lady nearly busted them rimming in the hot tub). They kissed. They fucked. They didn't talk about Jonny, or the PBC, that's for sure. They didn't even drink, and Michael was glad for the rest. Sometimes the sambuca and the beer and the occasional treats with Darcy were all too much. This was more like it, just sober sweaty naked fun.

"I haven't had a day like this in forever," he sighed as they lay in bed Friday night, legs intertwined, hands still roaming each other's bodies. "Matt, I..."

"Shhh. Don't say it," Matt said. "Let's not make this any more complicated than it needs to be."

"I do though."

"I do too."

"Oh! I don't want to go back to work tomorrow. It's just all so much, all the time. Plus, there's going to be so much gossip about this!"

"How are they going to know?"

"George finds out everything."

"Just don't tell him."

"He'll know when he sees me with you. I won't be able to keep my eyes or my hands off you."

"Your hands are feeling pretty good on me right now."

"Again? Wow, you're insatiable."

"I jerk off like four times a day if I'm not having sex."

"I don't think I've ever came this many times in so short a time."

"We have to go back to our regular lives tomorrow. Think you can handle one more?"

"Only if you're sitting on my face," Michael said, hands pulling Matt's legs apart.

"Deal. You're coming over to do this when we're back n Edmonton though. All the... time!"

"Mmmhmm," was the only answer Michael could give.

"Mmmhmmm, I don't think so, Michael!" George barked.

"Really! I spent the day puking."

"Well you better get your shit together. Stop drinking so much if you're going to be sick."

"OK OK."

"Now. Round of sambuca for me and my friend Matt here."

Michael poured out two shots. "And for you!" George barked. Michael poured a third. "Now Matt, thank you for driving my sick bartender here to work today. Cheers!" They tipped back the shots. "Are you guys just fucking or are you an item now?" Michael choked back up the licorice.

"You were right, Michael," Matt giggled. "How did you guess?"

"Honey, when you're as old as me, you've seen a lot of fags and they ain't hard to figure out. Now, Michael, you get Jonny and Adam down here tonight and let's be fucking grown-ups. We have a bar to run. Round of sambucas!"

"That is foul!" Michael said, slamming the shot glass down and gagging a little. "What was that?"

"Sambuca," Troy said. "You don't like?"

"I hate black licorice. I'll stick with tequila."

"Sorry, thought we'd try something new."

"Oh, it's all good. Here though, I need to get rid of the taste." Michael pulled Troy's face to his, licorice coated kisses. The pounding bass of the dance floor faded away. The lights dimmed. Just lips.

"Troy!"

Troy pulled back to see who was calling his name. She (he?) was 7 feet tall, long blond curls under a hat that must have been two feet wide, in a low cut lavender gown with a giant hoop skirt. Michael didn't know much about drag but this was a Queen from the Old South, conjuring up images of lazy plantation afternoons.

"Iona!" Troy practically squealed. "What brings you to town?"

"I have a paid gig tomorrow at the show here. I've moved to Edmonton actually. Vancouver was too much for me."

"Oh really? Michael here's from Edmonton. Michael, this is Iona Black. She used to live in Lethbridge."

"Long ago," she (he?) said, extending her hand to Michael, who took it and kissed the back of it awkwardly. "Enchanted to meet you, my darling." She turned back to Troy. "New boyfriend?"

Just then the DJ interrupted the music with a "Shooter Sale Shooter bar. For the next 15 minutes, Tequila $2.50". Michael missed Troy's answer entirely, as Iona took them both by the arms and said, "now come boys, buy an old Queen a drink."

Michael followed the old friends to the Shooter Bar, located in the back of Metro. The crowds of shirtless glistening men parted for the drag queen, all of whom seemed to know her, all of whom she greeted with a half wave.

"When you're Gay Bar Royalty," she explained, " they bend over backwards to please you, and sometimes," she added, "you bend over backwards to please them. And I'm very bendy." With that last, she grabbed Michael by the crotch and stepped in close, her (his?) voice dropping several octaves. Michael felt his face blush. "Oh, he's cute, Troy."

"Isn't he just?"

"Well, do come see my show tomorrow if you're not busy." She kissed Michael on his cheeks. Well, near both cheeks. Then did the same to Troy. Then she was off into the crowd, her wig and hat visible long after the rest of her was enveloped by the throng.

"Oh my god," Troy said. "I haven't seen her in years."

"You know him from Lethbridge?"

"He was just Darcy back then. 'Til he moved to Vancouver and found Iona in a hat box. Of such stories are legends born." Troy shook his head. "Great guy, big drug problem though."

"Oh?"

"Huge cokehead?"

"Have you ever tried it?"

"No! And don't you either! Drugs are bad."

"It doesn't interest me at all."

"Good," Troy yelled over the music. "Oh! Spice Girls! Let's dance."

"Let's dance!" Matt yelled.

"I can't. I'm working."

"You can take a break, it's dead."

It was, Michael thought. Far too often. A Saturday night, at midnight, and there were what? Thirty people. George was long gone. None of the PBC were still here. And with Matt batting his eyelashes over those beautiful eyes... "oh sure."

Matt put his hand on Michael's hip, grinding his hips against Michael. Michael could feel Matt start to get hard. Michael couldn't even imagine having sex again. After the previous three days (had it only been three days? Since Waldorf's funeral? Wow), plus all the shooters tonight, Michael just couldn't.

Where is Darcy with some treats, he thought. That would sober me up. Of course, coke dick wouldn't be very useful for fucking Matt.

Matt. Wow. Was this really happening? Arms in the air, bodies pressed tightly together. Damn, someone wants a drink. Oh it's just Princess Sophia. She can wait. This song is too good, this feels too good.

"And now let's slow things down with an oldie but a goodie," the DJ said.

Michael went to go back to the bar. "Let's slow dance," Matt said, grabbing his wrist. Enrique's Hero came on. "Would you dance if I asked you to dance," Matt sang along. Princess Sophia can definitely wait, Michael thought. Hands on each other's waists, they spun slowly, Matt's head resting comfortably on Michael's shoulder. A perfect fit. Lips met.

"This is completely inappropriate," Michael whispered.

"Yup." Matt smiled. Lips met.

They music faded, the dance floor lights faded, distant conversations muted.

Just Michael and Matt.

No cheating boyfriends. No dead princesses.

They song ended and they kept kissing. "Mmmm," Michael murmured as he broke away. "I have to get back to work."

"OK."

Off the dancefloor, there was Princess Sophia, tapping his foot impatiently. "About time, lovebirds."

"Round of sambuca!" Michael said, in his best George impression.

"Better pour one for Jonny too," Princess Sophia said.

Michael stopped in mid-pour. "Who...?"

"Yeah, he just went for a smoke. While you guys were dancing."

Oh. Fuck. Me. Michael thought.

"Fuck," Matt said, jumping off his bar stool, and tearing down the hallway.

"Maybe I'm good for shots tonight actually," Michael said, tipping his half-poured shot out.

"Cheers," Princess Sophia said, lifting his glass in salute. "And that's what you get for gossiping about me and William."

Oh. Fuck. Me.

"Fuck me, fuck me." Michael was on all fours, Troy behind him. "Harder, c'mon, harder!"

Troy let out a grunt and pulled out. Michael felt him shoot liquid fire on his back, just before he collapsed onto the bed next to him. Michael, panting, rolled onto his side, kissing Troy frantically, trying to get hard, trying to get off.

"What's wrong?"

"Nothing. It'll get there. Just... give me a minute... fuck!" Michael dropped onto his back, letting his flaccid dick alone. "I can do it."

"It's not a big deal Michael, it happens to everyone."

"Fuck."

"What's gotten into you tonight? You were insatiable."

Michael knew what it was. Well, suspected. And he couldn't tell Troy. *They'd been having so much fun at Metro, but he got too drunk, and he'd gone to the bathroom to puke, and there, he'd run into Iona, coming out of a stall. He splashed water onto his face, overwhelmed by shots. "Little drunk hun?" she asked*

"So wasted."

"Here, let Iona take care of you. I can fix that."

"Sure." He followed Iona into the stall. She took a small baggie from her bra, filled with white powder. *"Is that..."*

"It's wake-up dust," she said. *"It'll get you straightened out. Do you have a key?"*

Michael pulled his apartment key from his pocket. He shouldn't. But he wanted to keep having fun with Troy. He didn't want to just go back to Robert's. He sure didn't want to think about Robert being sick. Iona took the key, dipped it into the baggie, pulled it out with a small pile of the powder on the end. *"Cover your right nostril hun,"* she instructed as she raised the key to his left with a steady hand. *"Now breathe deep."*

White-gold fire flooded his brain. He choked, coughed, sneezed, shivered, flew.

"There you go, my boy," she said, *" you give that a few minutes. And don't tell Troy."*

His. Whole. Body. Vibrated. His. Pulse. Raced. Heart. Beat. Louder. The. Music. Popped. The. Lights. Were. Brighter. He. Sniffed. Hands. Shook. Dance. Dance. Troy. Dance. God. You. Feel. Good. Mmm. Lets. Go. Back. To. Roberts. I'm. So. Fucking. Horny.

"Fuck me."

He couldn't tell Troy. "You just make me so horny," he said, rolling on top of Troy and kissing him, their bodies slick and hot and young and beautiful. "Fuck me."

"Maybe in the morning, Michael. Go to sleep."

Michael gnawed at Troy's neck. "Seriously, Michael, go to sleep."

"You feel so good."

"What the fuck, dude? Are you on something?" Michael bit Troy's nipple. "You are, aren't you?" Troy pushed Michael up and grabbed hold of his face. "Look at me."

"Yes. Sorry. Iona said it would sober me up so we could keep having a good time."

"Fuck, Michael! I just told you how much I hate drugs. Fuck. I told you specifically not to do coke. Fucking Darcy! He knows I hate that shit." Troy jumped out of bed and pulled on his jeans. "I'm sleeping on the couch. Fuck!" He slammed the door behind him.

Michael lay naked on the bed, alone, in the dark. His chest heaving, dry lips, heart pounding. "Fuck me." He started to sob.

The Princess Bar had seen a lot of tears over the years. Fucking faggot drama queens, as George would put it, even though a lot of the drama was instigated by him. George found nothing more enjoyable than feeding people liquor then setting off a domestic quarrel with just a few words. Then it was simply time to sit back, sip his Rum and Coke, and watch the show. The progressively messier, increasingly louder, and Sambuca-fed show.

Unfortunately for George, he was gone home early the night Jonny and Matt broke up messily, loudly, and in the parking lot. Michael and the few patrons in the bar tried to watch while trying not to watch. People coming in from smoke breaks brought status updates on the relationship tailspin, and the squeal of Jonny's tires signaled the end.

"I'm staying at your place," Matt said to Michael. "Jonny is moving his stuff out tomorrow but I don't even want to be there."

"Sure, Matt. Of course. You don't even have to ask.

"When are you done? I'm exhausted. I hate drama."

"I'm doing last call right now," he said, "Last Call!" he yelled.

"It's only 1:30," Rick said.

"You don't need anymore anyway, Princess."

"I'll have three doubles then."

"Fuck off, Rick. No way I'm staying here all night just so you can get even more shit-faced and annoying."

"Too much drama interfering with your job, hey? I'm sure George will love to hear about it."

"Oh, don't worry about it, Michael. I'll just go home and sleep on the couch," Matt said.

"No really, Matt, I..."

"Never mind, I'm going," Matt slammed back his gin. "I'll talk to you later."

"But.."

But Matt was gone.

"Can I get those doubles now?"

"Fuck you, Rick, you're done."

"You can't cut me off."

"Pretty sure I just did. Get a cab. You're done."

"Nope. I'm staying 'til the end."

"Oh my god, Rick, go home!" Michael was practically screaming, practically sobbing in frustration.

-Youre an asshole-

-for what Jonny?-

"Double please."

"Go home."

-stealing my boyfriend-

"A shooter then?"

"Oh my god, if I give you a shooter will you just go home?"

"Yes."

-I did not. You guys were done-

Michael poured Rick a shot. He tipped it back, wobbling. "Can I have a drink please?"

"Ah!"

-we would have worked it out. He cheated, I cheated. It was even. 'Til you messed things up-

"Is that a no?"

"Yes, it's a no. Go home!"

"OK." Rick stumbled outside.

-I cant control what you guys did to each other Jonny- Jonny-with-the-hot-ass-and-hotter-boyfriend, Michael thought.

-oh my god Matt, Jonny's being an ass-

"Did you call me a cab?"

"Call one yourself Rick! There's a cab phone right there!"

-falling in love with someone else's boyfriend is pretty low buddy-

-whatever Jonny. Leave me alone-

Michael turned off his phone, then realized Matt wouldn't be able

to text him back, and turned it back on. He sat staring at the phone, waiting for it to ring as he listened to Rick try to order a cab. The DJ shut down the music. No text. He cashed out. No text.

Fuck I wish I'd gotten some blow after all, he thought, as he turned off the lights and locked the door. What a fucking trainwreck.

Even without coke, sleep eluded him. And all the while, his phone lay there silent.

When he woke in the morning, Michael grimaced as he reached for his phone, then grimaced again when he saw the first text was from Jonny.

-ha. Sux 2 b u-

-wtf?-

And then he saw the text from Matt. - so Jonny and I are going to try to work things out-

-WTF-

-Four years is a lot to throw away-

-it is but I thought we had something-

-we do. I like being naked with you. And I told Jonny that's not going to stop-

-so what? He's your boyfriend and I'm what? Your mistress?-

-well, my mister-

-haha-

-no drama Michael-

-k-

Some days, Michael thought, it's just not worth waking up.

When he woke in the morning, Michael grimaced. His head pounded. His ass hurt. His dick chafed. His mouth was dry.

And Troy wasn't in the bed next to him.

Nervously, he got dressed and went out to the kitchen. Robert was sitting in his breakfast nook, reading the paper, sipping his coffee. "Good morning."

"Hi."

"Quite a night you had, hey?"

"Yah. Sorry if we woke you."

"Well, I didn't mind getting woken by the fucking," Robert said. "Frankly, it's time this house saw some action. The fighting however..."

"Sorry."

"I don't suppose I need to lecture you on how stupid and dangerous drugs are."

"Please don't. Where's Troy?"

"He went home, Michael."

"He what?"

"He got up early and asked if I'd mind driving you back. He didn't want to see you."

"What the fuck?"

"He's really mad and hurt, Michael. Have some breakfast."

"I can't eat. I can't fucking believe this happened."

"You really messed up, Michael."

"It was one time. One stupid time. He's overreacting, don't you think?"

"You need to talk to him about that. He has his reasons, Michael. Now, if you're not going to eat, then let's get you home."

Some days, Michael thought, it's just not worth waking up.

His name was Kirk, the note under Michael's door began. When we were talking about everything under the sun yesterday, I didn't mention him. We were avoiding exes. Maybe I should have. But I didn't. Kirk was 17 when I met him. I was 19. I'd been out for a whole year so I thought I knew all about being gay. How wrong I was Michael. Kirk came out when he was 15. To his crazy Christian family. His dad beat the shit out of him and kicked him out of the house. You'd think it would be hard for a 15-year-old in Lethbridge to find drugs but no. By the time I met him, he had a full blown coke problem. He was so beautiful, despite the twitchiness. I was sure I could save him. I let him move in with me, to get him clean. And it worked and when he looked at me with his soulful sober brown eyes, he shone like an angel. I came home one day to find those soulful brown eyes open and empty and dead. He'd been clean for two months and it still hadn't fixed what was broken. He'd overdosed on my bedroom floor and everything that shone in him was gone. I'm disgusted that you did it, and that you came to our bed like a druggy slut. You didn't even want me. You just wanted cock. Drugs kill, Michael. Not only will they kill you, they'll kill any chance of an us. I don't know if I can get over this. Don't call me. I'll call you when I can.

Michael folded up the letter. "Stupid stupid stupid," he said. The morning after getting fucked, he always felt a void where they'd been. This was different, bigger, worse. It was a great big empty in his chest. "Stupid stupid stupid."

"Pretty stupid, Michael. This does not sound like it's going to end well."

"But LBP, it's Matt. You know how long I've wanted hm."

"You're going to get hurt. He can't have his cake and eat you too."

"He thinks he can."

"And Jonny's fine with this?"

"Supposedly, Jonny can do other people too."

"It won't end well."

"We'll see."

"Pretty stupid, Michael."

"Thanks Genie."

"Why would you try coke from some random drag queen in a bathroom?"

"It seemed like a good idea at the time."

"I can't imagine how. So has Troy called yet?"

"No, and it's been a week. I think I fucked it up."

"I think so too, but I guess we'll see."

-**A**re you coming down tonight-

-be there in 10. you have treats?-

-absolutely Darcy, it's our line-i-versary haha-

-haha have them ready haha-

Michael gave the bar a quick glance. Everyone was fully cocktailed: LBP, Nelly Belle, a sheepish Princess Sophia (embarrassed by his behavior the prior Saturday). George was in the office. Perfect timing.

In stall 2, and just to be funny, Michael set up a tea light candle in a cute glass holder, framed nicely by two lines of coke. As he waited for Darcy, he sniffed back a bit of his, felt that familiar burn. It had been a couple weeks since they'd partaken, what with Waldorf passing and all the Matt sex.

The door to the washroom opened. Michael peered through the partition and recognized Darcy's coat. He opened the door, passed Darcy the rolled-up bill.

"Oooh a fifty."

"Classy I know."

"Thank you." SNIFF. "You go."

SNIFF. "Yummy."

"I can't believe it's been fifteen years since our first bump."

"Well, I didn't do any for 11 of those," Michael said.

"Oh, me neither," Darcy laughed. "How am I?"

"Good. Me?"

"Good."

"Beer then?"

"Yes."

Darcy held the door open for Michael. "I still feel bad about that."

"No, you don't."

"No, I don't. But I should."

"Troy and I wouldn't have lasted anyway. Hell, he ended up moving to Toronto a few months later anyway."

"You never know though. Oh, that was good!"

"New source."

"Ah. And how are things with Matt?" Darcy asked as they sat down.

"It won't end well," LBP said.

"So you keep saying."

"Well, it's true, Michael."

"Maybe."

"Where is Matt anyway?" Darcy asked.

"It's his Jonny night. He only hangs out with Michael here on Mondays and Wednesdays."

"How scheduled."

"It won't end well."

"Oh shut up, Little Buddy."

"Sambucas please!" George came sauntering down the hall.

Michael leapt to his feet and grabbed the Luxardo from the cooler.

"Not me," Princess Sophia said.

George snorted. "If you can't drink with the big dogs, don't go in the yard."

"He's the boss," Michael said, pouring the round. The door opened and heads all turned as Adam walked in. Michael added an extra shot.

"Here comes trouble!" George yelled.

"Hi."

"Your usual, Adam?"

"Thanks, Michael."

"And where have you been hiding?" LBP asked.

"Busy with work."

"Sure..." George said in his knowing George way. "Drink up bitches." Sambucas went up, glasses came down. "Fuck I'm gorgeous!"

Half an hour later, Darcy met Michael's eyes and Michael nodded the barely perceptible nod that meant "Look acknowledged, more blow coming". He wiped up the 'buca spillage, sticky on the bar like half-dry cum, and then, looking around, said, "be right back. Need to pee."

Moments later, in the bathroom, as Michael got up from where he straddled the toilet with a great SNIFF and shiver, he heard someone come in.

"All yours, Darc."

"It's Adam."

"Oh. Uhm..."

"I don't care. You should quit that though."

"I know. It's just once in a while."

"Like a Thursday at 6?"

"Yah, I guess." He covered the remaining with a small scrap of toilet paper and went to the sink. Adam was at the stall peeing.

"So uhm... I'm sorry about everything."

"Not your fault. Not really."

"We good?"

"Yah, Michael. We're good."

Michael opened the door to leave.

"You never answered my text by the way."

Michael paused. "That's right, I didn't."

"Does that mean no?"

"No. It just got overlooked with everything."

As he washed his hands, Adam said, "I like you, Michael. You're a nice guy. Bit of a mess though."

"Sometimes." Michael chuckled nervously.

"Yeah. Sometimes."

"Well, I'm going home. Text me."

"You didn't finish your drink."

"Don't even want it. I just came to see you."

"Oh."

"Good night Michael." As Adam passed by Michael on his way out of the bathroom, he squeezed Michael's hand, briefly, tightly., Then he was gone and Darcy caught the door as it swung shut.

"Everything ok?"

"Yah. It's waiting for you."

"What did Adam want?"

"I'm really not sure," Michael said. Adam with the dimples and the curls. "I'm not sure."

"I'm not sure, Michael. I'm still so angry."

"It's been over a week, Troy. I'm sorry. If I'd known how upset you'd be, I never would have done it."

"See? You shouldn't have done it because it's dangerous and stupid. Not just so you didn't upset me."

"I was drunk. I wasn't thinking."

"And what happens next time you're drunk?"

"It was your friend."

"Who I told you specifically had a drug problem that I told you I hated."

"I just wish none of this ever happened."

"Me too."

"Can't you ever forgive me?"

"I can forgive you, sure. I just don't know if I can ever trust you again."

"I swear Troy. I swear that I will never touch cocaine again." A pause. "I miss you."

A pause. "I miss you too."

A longer pause. Sniff away the tears. "Come over?"

"I have an early flight tomorrow, Michael. I'll call you when I get back."

"Troy, I..."

"Don't say it."

"I do though."

"No you don't, Michael. It's too soon. And if you did, you never would have betrayed me like this." A pause. "I'll call you when I get back. Goodbye, Michael."

"Goodbye Troy."

Just as "hello" at the Princess Bar would often take the form of "here comes trouble", "speaking of cunts...", or "look what the tranny dragged in", "goodbye" at the Princess Bar was said a variety of ways too. A smack on the ass, a kiss on the cheek, a grope to the crotch, were some of the physical ones. "Good riddance", "about fucking time", or "your cab's here" were some of the verbal ones.

Princess Sophia Maria Victoria Secret said goodbye another way entirely.

"Fuck, Rick, you're gonna get cut off again," Michael snapped. "Seriously dude, what the fuck. This is two Saturdays in a row."

"What's your fucking rush? Not like you're going to sleep with Matt tonight. He's with Jonny. HIS BOYFRIEND."

"That's none of your..."

"Not like you're going to sleep at all, you fucking cokehead."

Michael felt his jaw drop. "What did you say?"

"Everyone fucking knows it. You and Darcy think you're so subtle and clever. You're fucking not."

"Dude, you're crossing a line."

"You're a fucking joke, Michael. A fucking joke!" Rick threw his drink across the bar, ice bouncing across the counter.

"You're fucking done!"

"I wouldn't fucking drink here again anyway. Druggy whores and fags. I'm gone!" His ricochets off the wall marred his grand exit but Michael was too stunned to laugh.

"Where the hell did that come from?" Nelly Belle asked.

"I have no fucking clue. He's done though. I'm not serving him again."

"George never bars regulars."

"He fucking will now or I'm gone." Michael was vibrating. "You good for Last Call, Nelly?"

"Yah."

"I'll be back."

Michael went into stall 2, still vibrating. Fucking Princess Sophia, who does she think she is? His hands shook so badly, he could barely open the little baggy. This isn't a problem, just a bit of fun. Steadily, he poured a small pile into the little pocket between his thumb and finger. It's not like I need this, he thought, as he lifted his hand to his nostril and inhaled. MMM. Well maybe I needed that. MMM.

As he looked into the mirror, checking for a telltale white ring, he stared himself in the face. Who the fuck does that alcoholic old fag think he is, judging me. I'm not a cokehead. Stupid drunk.

He dumped out another small pile, and as the white fire filled his brain, he thought, well... maybe...

"Look what the tranny dragged in!" George hollered as Michael walked into the bar Monday at 4.

"Fucking rights." Michael paused. "You can't say tranny anymore though."

"I'll say whatever the fuck I want. It's just a word."

"OK, but if you piss off some activists, don't come crying to me, old man."

"So, tell me a story. What happened Saturday after I left?"

Fuck gossip travels in this stupid city. "Rick was a drunk mess again. If he can't learn to maintain, I'm not putting up with him screaming at me."

"That's what I pay you to do."

"Nope. He's over the top."

"Why? What's he done?"

"He can't even walk by the end of the night."

"Good. Pays my rent."

"No, not good. He pisses off other customers then they go to Divas."

"Well, I'll talk to him."

"No! I don't want to serve him."

"Then there's the door."

Michael, fuming, started setting up the bar in silence. George sat there, as Michael stomped and slammed about. "Change your attitude!" Michael ignored him, finishing. "Unlock the door, and change your attitude now!"

Michael unlocked the door and grabbed a bucket of hot water. He scrubbed at a wall while George sat there. The awkwardness and tension hung heavily in the air. The door opened.

"Here comes trouble!" George yelled as a greeting to Darcy.

"Good afternoon! Beer please!"

Michael dropped his rag heavily into the bucket, water splashing out. He cracked a beer, dropped it in front of Darcy, went back to his bucket.

"What's going on?"

"Princess here is having a tantrum."

"Oh fuck off, George."

"Change your tone!"

Michael rolled his eyes and went to the bathroom, where he

leaned against the wall and tapped his foot in frustration. He could hear George howling in laughter at one of his own stories, heard the door open.

"Princess Sophia!" George yelled.

Oh for fuck sake, Michael thought, jaw clenched, lips pursed. What was it about George that sent him into these stupid pouts! George is in the wrong! Fuck!

Darcy came in. "What's going on?"

"Fucking Rick was a drunk prick on Saturday. I don't want to serve him."

"George has already. What did he say?"

"Oh, apparently, you and I are big drug addicts and everyone talks about it."

"Let them talk."

"And he doesn't fucking listen to me. I'm the one that has to be here 'til close, dealing with all the stupid drunks after he stumbles his fat ass home."

"It's his bar, Michael."

"I know. Just... fuck!"

"Want a treat?"

"No. I'm good. Thanks anyway."

Darcy went into the stall and Michael heard the rustling, heard the plastic on porcelain that meant an Iona-sized line was being cut, the big sniff, the fake flush.

Maybe it is pretty obvious, he thought.

"Ok, let's go have a shooter," Darcy said.

"Fine." They left the bathroom. "Round of sambuca!" Michael hollered.

"That's better," George said.

"Michael!" Genie yelled down the hall. "Phone! It's Troy!"

That's better, Michael thought. Knew he'd come around. Deep breath. "Hello?"

"Hi Michael."

"Hey Troy. How was your flight?"

"It was good. What are you doing?"

"Studying. It's finals soon."

"Oh."

"Why? What's up?"

"Think you can take a study break?"

"Sure. Did you want to do something?"

"I'll come over. Better in person," Troy hung up.

Or not better, Michael thought, closing his eyes and banging his forehead with his fists. Stupid stupid stupid.

It wasn't what Michael thought though. In a way, it was much worse. A job transfer? Who'd seen that coming? But it was too good an opportunity to pass up (apparently) and had nothing to do with what had happened in Calgary (sure) and Michael could come visit in Toronto anytime (uh huh), and there were still a couple months...

"No," Michael said. "If you're moving, I can't spend two months pretending you're not. Better we call it quits now before I feel more than I'm already feeling."

"If that's what you want..."

"It is. I need to study."

"OK. Call me later."

"Bye, Troy."

"Goodbye, Michael."

The Homohop was as close to a gay bar as Lethbridge came. Eight times a year, the local gay group rented out a hall, threw up some streamers, and stocked it with beer, vodka, and Spice Girls. Think junior high school dance meets wedding reception with a rainbow flag.

Still, for 'bridge boys and Lethbians, it was a social highlight, and Michael always looked forward to them, flask of tequila in hand. This one though, not so much. It was Troy's Going Away HomoHop and it was 12:30 already and Troy wasn't there and there were so many things Michael wanted to say.

Once, in the past two months, they'd gotten together for coffee, which became dinner, which became breakfast. Awkward and amazing all at the same time. Between finals for Michael, packing for Troy, and then packing for Michael when Genie and Jamie decided to get their own place, thereby bumping Michael into a bachelor, even that one awkward amazing night was lucky to get.

All day before Troy's Going Away HomoHop, Michael daydreamed of that one last perfect night. Slow dancing. Kisses in the moonlight. Falling asleep in Troy's arms. And now, here it was, 12:45, and no Troy. Where was Troy?

And then there he was. That Jordan Catalano hair, Those piercing blue eyes. That soft pink lipped smile. His pilot God. Michael pushed his way across the floor. Didn't those old men and women realize he was down to hours with Troy? Only hours?

"Hi." That's not what he'd meant to say. He meant to say I love you, don't go.

"Hi." That's not what he was meant to say. He was supposed to say I love you, come with me.

"Your last dance."

"Haha yah."

"I was starting to think you wouldn't show."

"Lots of last minute stuff to do."

"I bet." There wasn't supposed to be this uncomfortable awkwardness. Where was all the amazing?

"I'm going to get a drink."

"OK." Should he go with him to the bar? "I'll be around."

"OK."

Michael watched Troy get a drink.

Michael watched Troy do the rounds.

Michael watched Troy say goodbye to friends.

Michael watched Troy.

Oh, there were some brief eye contact and smiles across the room. But that was it. And then suddenly...

"All right everyone. This will be your last song of the night." And predictably, it was Celine, belting out the love theme from Titanic.

Slowly, through the crowd, Troy walked towards hm. "Dance with me?" he said, with hand extended.

His heart in his throat, Michael took Troy's hand and they circled in silence. It was short, it was sweet, and when it was done, they looked at each other with wet eyes.

"I'm going to miss you."

"I'll write."

"You better."

"Take care, Michael."

Michael watched Troy walk away.

Michael watched Troy leave the hall.

Michael watched Troy leave the parking lot.

"Goodbye, Troy."

"That was awesome, Matt," Michael said, as he rolled onto his back, sweating, panting.

"Mmm." Matt rolled onto Michael and kissed him. "K I gotta go."

"What? Really?"

"Meeting Jonny for dinner."

"Really."

"Yah. It's our five-year anniversary."

"And you thought you'd celebrate with a quick post-work fuck with your mistress?"

"Yah, wonderful isn't it?" Matt flashed that impossible-to-stay-mad-at grin and Michael melted.

"Guess I shouldn't complain."

"Nope."

"Where you guys going?" Michael asked as Matt got dressed.

"Normands, I think."

"Cool. Well, you guys have a nice time."

Matt leaned in and gave Michael another kiss. "Thanks babe. See you on the weekend."

"I'll be here," Michael said, as Matt left the room. "Waiting," he added to himself. This isn't going to end well, he thought.

Three months.

Three months of mind-shattering orgasms and sweaty naked fun. Three months of sweet Matt kisses and that look in his blue-green eyes that Michael knew (KNEW) meant Matt was as much in love with Michael as Michael was with Matt.

Three months of Matt going home to Jonny as Michael lay in bed alone.

And as Michael fell deeper and deeper, he knew (KNEW) that one day, there would be no Jonny. It would be just him and Matt.

Together.

Forever.

One day.

But until then, Michael thought as he reached for his phone -hey Adam, whats up, want to grab some dinner?-

It was a stupid stupid stupid idea, Michael knew (KNEW) that, but it still didn't stop him. Sometimes, the drama made things all the more exciting, forced the intimacy to speed up, plus the food was really good, so when Michael met Adam outside Normands for dinner, it didn't seem so stupid stupid stupid.

"Hey, Michael." A quick hug. "I'm glad you texted."

"Me too. Ever been here?"

"Nope."

"It's good. Hope you're hungry."

"Starved actually," Adam smiled, holding the door open.

"For two please," Michael greeted the maitre-d.

As they were led to their table, Adam said, in a whisper, "is that Matt and Jonny?"

"Why, so it is."

"Awkward."

"A bit."

"Oh well, small world."

"Very."

When Jonny happened to see them, and Adam gave a half wave, and Michael pretended not to see them, and then Matt came over, STUPID STUPID STUPID ran through Michael's head again.

"Mind if I talk to you for a minute outside, Mikey?"

"Uhm sure, Matt, excuse me. If he comes, I'll have the elk," he told Adam.

Outside, Matt asked, "what the hell, Michael?"

"What? When you mentioned it, I thought it sounded good for dinner."

"With Adam."

"Yah."

"You're fucked up man."

"It's not awkward for me."

"Oh really? Good, you can join us then."

What? "What?"

"Oh sure, why not. The more the fucking merrier."

Inside, Michael and Adam moved to the table next to Matt and Jonny, pushing them together even as Matt whispered to Jonny, calming the purpling rage on his face.

"Can we get a bottle of the house red?" Matt asked a passing server. "And if you have sambuca, we'd love a round of shots."

Before the naked cheating lying fighting started, they had all been friends, the young corner of the PBC. Over a bottle of wine, it was easy to pretend like none of those ill-gotten orgasms had happened, easy to pretend that Matt hadn't left Michael's bed to go to his anniversary dinner, easy to pretend that Jonny wasn't still furious with Michael and Adam both, easy to pretend that Michael wasn't hopelessly in love.

They drank. They laughed. They ate. They drank. They laughed. They drank. They decided to go to Divas to go dancing.

"Round of sambuca?" Matt asked, as they sat in the booth, pitcher of beer and 4 glasses on the table between them. "Adam, come help me carry."

"Sure." They left.

"So Jonny..."

"You're a fuck up, Michael. I'm so mad at you."

Matt and Adam were laughing at the bar.

"I'm sorry, Jonny. Can we get past this?"

"No."

"Shooters!" Matt said, dropping the shots onto the table. "Cheers!" Bucas up, glasses down. "Oh! I love this song! Let's dance." He grabbed Jonny's hand. "Are you guys coming?"

"I'm good here," Michael said, pouring some more beer.

"I'll dance," Adam said, and then the three of them were off. Michael drained his glass, refilled it. Look at them dancing, he thought. Matt is so beautiful. Fucking lucky Jonny, he thought as Jonny ground his crotch into Matt's butt. God I love him. He drained another glass of draft. God, this does down too fast, I'm hammed. What. The. Fuck.

It was slow motion.

The rest of the club melted away and all there was was Matt, Jonny still tight behind him, pulling Adam in close, and What. The. Fuck. Matt was kissing Adam, then Jonny. Then Jonny was kissing Adam.

Close your eyes Michael, Michael told himself. Block the images away. Too late. Seared into your brain, etched there like a summer sun. Blinding and painful. Open up your eyes, in time to see the three of them, going up the stairs and out the door!

They'll be back. Just fresh air. They're not... they wouldn't... they couldn't...

Michael picked up the pitcher and drained what was left. Stupid stupid stupid!

-did you guys leave- drunk text to Matt.

-where are you- drunk text to Adam.

-who's the asshole now- drunk text to Jonny

-don't call me-drunker text to Adam.

-we're done-drunker text to Matt.

Buca up, glass down. Buca up glass down.

-are you awake-drunk text to Darcy.

-I love you-drunk text to Matt.

-can I get a half-drunk text to dealer

Buca up, glass down. Oh! Buca coming back up!

After puking up the foamy pale yellow draft-buca bile, it's time to go, Michael thought. No Drugs. Fuck.

-I thought you liked me-drunk text to Adam.

-fgyck tyio-drunk text to Matt.

-be there in 20-from dealer.

-am at Divas-

-oh, am outside-

Michael stumbled outside, around back, saw the car, knocked on

the window. $40 in, baggie out. Dump out a bump right there. Hey that rhymes. Dump a bump haha. MMMM. Sobers you right up. Time for more beer. Buca up glass down. Bump. Buca. Beer. Beer. Bump. Buca. Bump.

Everything goes hazy. Everything but that threeway dancefloor kiss. Are they still going? It is still a tangle of limbs and cock and lips and lust? Slut! Fucking sluts! Fuck I'm so alone! Fucking cokehead! Fuck fuckety fuck fuck fuck.

Michael woke up at three. "Fuck." Into fresh-smelling clothes and out the door to work.

"You look like hell," George barked.

"Ugh."

"Long night?"

"You could say that."

"Why didn't you answer your phone this afternoon?"

"You called?"

"You're training tonight."

"Ugh. I can't."

"If you can't lift your leg with the big dogs, then don't piss in the yard."

"That doesn't even make sense George."

"Shuddup! Fuck I'm gorgeous," George yelled, and he laughed so hard he began to cough. "Sambuca!"

Michael poured the shots. Buca up. "Ugh." Hard to swallow. Glass down. Crack a breakfast beer. Ah that's better. Discreetly check pockets. Good. Baggie isn't empty. Just get through this shift. What a blur. Only six hours. I can do this. What the fuck was that last night!

And then there was that image again. A daisy chain of dance floor kissing. And scattered other images out of the fog. Drunken texts. Ack. Puking. Ugh. Did I really do a bump right at the bar? Fuck. Oh God. Fuck Michael. Stupid stupid stupid.

The new guy was called Greg, and when he walked into Lethbridge gay coffee, there were no fireworks. He was average. Not hot, not ugly, just average. Plus, it had only been two months since Troy left. Two months that Michael had spent in his new bachelor pad, focusing on school, where the only social interaction he had was on the gay #IRC channels.

Still, Greg was younger than most so Michael invited him to sit at the "kids table", where the college kids, etc, hung out. Michael, Genie and Jamie, Sherry and Evan, David (still awkward there), Mario and Jared, Jen and Kate and Terri, Ryan and Brian, the "gang".

Greg was twenty-four, and just out. Crazy Mormon mothers, he said, didn't make for easy coming out. Crazy mothers Michael could understand, and they shared crazy mother stories and laughed.

"Wow. Is that the time?" Michael said, looking at his watch. "It's after ten." He looked around, the place was pretty cleared out. "I should be getting home."

"Need a ride?" Greg asked.

Michael looked at him. His eyes were a pretty sparkling green. "Sure."

Outside Michael's little apartment, he asked "Did you want to come in?"

"No. Not tonight. I'd like to call you though."

"Oh. Sure." They exchanged numbers and then Greg drove off, not even a kiss goodnight.

For the best, Michael thought, I'm done with men anyway.

The new guy was called Luc, and when he walked into Choices for his training shift, it was to a chorus of catcalls from the PBC. Why, Michael couldn't see, but he'd never gone for the beefy, tatted type (maybe shades of Scott), and besides, the agony of hangover had sex the last thing on his mind.

Training at the PBC was a simple thing. "This is LBP, he drinks Rum and Diet. This is Princess Sophia, Rye and 7. Darcy drinks Bud. This is Statler, he'll have a large pitcher. This is George, he's a cunt but he signs our checks so a round of sambucas."

"Liquor comes from here. Money goes there. Ask if you have questions." And then Michael sat and drank and rehydrated and snuck in a few bumps, not party bumps, just small ones to keep him going.

Five hours to go.

Four.

"Here comes trouble!" George yelled, and Michael turned his head with the rest of the PBC.

Jonny and Matt. And Adam.

Fuck.

"Good evening boys. This is Jonny, Canadian. Matt, gin and tonic. Adam, gin and 7."

"And a round of sambuca!"

Michael sat back down as Luc poured the drinks. If he focused on Luc's pouring, he didn't have to see the smug expression on Jonny's face, or the indifferent ones on Matt and Adam's, or the casual touch of a hand on a shoulder or a leg. Focusing his attention couldn't block out Matt's giggle though, or the image of those dance floor kisses.

Time for a real bump, he thought. Fuck, and that's all there is. Three hours to go. I can do, he told himself, checking his reflection in the mirror. God. What a mess. Who would want me?

The door opened and in came Matt.

"How are you?"

"Been better, Matt, been better."

"It was a stupid thing to do, Michael."

"So what was it? A revenge threeway?"

"Maybe a little. You could've come if you didn't always have to make things mean so much."

"You know how I feel."

"And you know I don't like drama."

"Taking Adam home wasn't drama?"

"Taking Adam home was fun. And you could've joined in."

"No, I don't think I could have."

"Damn it, Michael." Matt grabbed him by the wrist. Now there'd be a kiss and everything would be better. Michael closed his eyes.

"You've got coke on your nose." Matt let go and walked out.

Michael stared into the mirror, that little white clump on the inside of his nostril. The harder he stared, the more his face seemed to melt into that white. His hands clenched. "Fuck."

Darcy came in. "Treat?"

"Yes!" When you're flying high enough, nothing can touch you.

"Round of sambuca!" Michael ordered. "Me and these three boys right here." Luc poured the shots, brought them over to Michael, Matt, Jonny, Adam. "Put them on LBP's tab!" Michael laughed.

"I don't think so, bitch! Pay for your own shooters!"

"Boo!" Michael laughed and gave Luc a $20. "Throw the rest in your jar. Shots up boys." Buca up, glass down. Ugh, that one was hard. "Fuck I'm gorgeous!"

"Channelling your inner George, hey?" Matt said.

"You know it, Princess."

They drank. They laughed. Michael knew he was overcompensating, knew it was the coke talking and laughing, knew it didn't matter. He had to fix things with Matt. They had to be good again. Had it only been a day? How were things so strained?

"Luc's hot," Matt said.

"What? Really?" Jonny said.

"Yeah. The shaved head, the tats."

"I didn't know that's what you go for," Michael said, suddenly picturing himself bald and inked and stealing Matt from Jonny.

"That's the porn I watch." Michael suddenly pictured Matt watching porn, jerking off, head thrown back, hand a blur.

"Michael, can you come here?" Luc called from the bar.

"Be right back."

As Michael explained how to change a keg, he said without thinking, "Matt thinks you're hot."

"Which one's Matt again?"

"Gin tonic."

"Oh he's cute. Single?"

"No. He's dating Jonny but they're open."

"Oh. Good to know. Thanks bro."

Bro? Who is this guy? Kevin Kosinski?

Back at the table, Michael said, "Luc thinks you're cute."

"Really?" Matt tipped back his drink. "Be right back."

"What are you doing Michael?" Jonny asked.

"Setting your boyfriend up on a date."

"You're a fucking idiot, you know that right?"

Suddenly, Michael saw Matt laughing with Luc at the bar, saw Jonny glaring at him, saw Adam looking at him with what? Sympathy? Disgust? Some kind of judgment anyway. Well, fuck him.

"Fuck you, Jonny."

Jonny shook his head, finished his drink. Michael watched him go up to Matt, watched Matt shake his head, giggling that Matt giggle. His hand was on Luc's. Jonny stormed back to their table.

"Did you want a ride home, Adam? Matt's staying, I guess."

"He doesn't have to go home just because you're having a tantrum."

As Jonny sputtered, Adam said, "no, I think I will"

"But..."

"Not impressed, Michael."

Michael watched Jonny and Adam leave, Jonny's arms around Adam's waist. Michael watched Matt flirt with Luc.

He took his beer up to the bar and sat down next to LBP. "This isn't going to end well," he said.

"That's what I've been trying to tell you."

"It's just not fun anymore."

"Sounds like a lot of fun," Greg said.

"Oh it has been. Maybe too much," Michael laughed. "We had people over every weekend. Got a bit tiring to be honest. I wasn't completely horrified when she said she was moving out."

"And that was right after you and Troy broke up?"

"Pretty much. So it was a new apartment and no boyfriend all at once."

"Big changes."

"I've really been focusing on school."

"How long do you have left again?"

"If I take summer session again this year, I'll be done in December, but don't get to convocate 'til March."

So far away, Michael thought. Yet so close. He let his mind drift.

That was one of the good things about Greg. He didn't always have to talk, and when Michael's mind wandered, Greg just sat there and waited for Michael to come back to Earth.

They'd been hanging out almost every day for three weeks, and nothing had happened. Boardgames and movies and dinner. Maybe Greg did just want to be friends. Probably for the best. Michael still couldn't decide if he was attracted or not.

Too bad though. He was so sweet.

And he did have pretty eyes.

"I so don't want to go home for Easter," Michael said. "I've got so much to do. And it's such a rushed trip."

"You'll be back before you know it. Going to go out while you're home?"

"I don't know anyone in Edmonton to go out with." Just Iona, he thought, and I don't know how to get a hold of her. Or even if I'd want to.

"Can always go out by yourself."

"True. Maybe, We'll see this weekend I guess."

"When does your bus leave?"

"Seven."

"I'll already be at work."

"Poor you."

"I should go and let you pack."

"You don't have to."

"OK."

"But I do have to pack," Michael said. "It won't take long. We can watch a movie after."

"Sounds good."

Greg just sat there as Michael packed. He's so quiet, Michael thought. So different from me. Clothes went into the suitcase, disc-man, some CDs, some textbooks. Then he sat down on the couch and they put on a movie. Somehow, as they watched, their feet ended up brushing against each other. Greg pulled away. They did again, and this time he didn't. Michael felt Greg's toes barely caress the arch of his foot. He wasn't really watching the movie now, and there was suddenly this electricity in the air. His toes bumped into Greg's thigh. Then Greg's hand was on Michael's calf, his fingers brushing his knee, his thigh. Michael shifted on the couch. Those fingers felt too good and it had been too long.

"Can I come up to your end?" Greg asked.

"Sure."

And then Greg was behind him, arm around Michael's waist. Michael could feel that Greg was every bit as hard as he was. Greg's fingers were playing with Michael's hair, his left hand sliding up Michael's T-shirt. Michael let out a small moan and thrust his hips. Greg's hand hit Michael's belt then was back out of his shirt.

Oh come on! Michael thought, as he ground his ass back into Greg's crotch. Michael's left hand was behind him, pulling Greg into him. Greg's breath was warm and sweet on Michael's neck.

Had he ever been this hard?

Greg's hand hit Michael's belt again and this time, he didn't flinch. Michael flexed his dick through his jeans, felt Greg's jump in reaction. Michael rolled around, face to face, cock to cock, lips met, hesitantly then with a frenzy.

They made out for what seemed like hours, hands roaming. The insistent need below went unmet, as kissing built and built and then finally, hands were undoing belts and with lips never parting, it was hands on dicks, the heat, the sweat, the thrusting, and then the exploding release all the while their lips never parted.

"Sorry," Greg said, as they were wiping up. "Guess I got carried away."

Michael laughed nervously. "It's OK. We both did."

"I should go."

"OK."

"Talk to you when you get back."

Michael locked the door behind him, and, sated, fell asleep.

"George! How are you?"

"Well, I'll tell you, Michael, I'm better than a handjob!"

Michael laughed as he poured drinks for George and old Ralph, George's frail yet feisty friend up from the Okanagan.

"Indeed!" Ralph said, "I'd've figured you'd just take your teeth out and give them a gummer."

"Bitch!"

"George hasn't had any in years," Michael said.

"That's because of his dickdoitis, where his belly sticks out farther than his dick do."

"Round of sambucas!" George yelled, banging his fist on the bar as Ralph and Michael laughed. "You cunts!"

It was a small round, George and Ralph, the ever present LBP, and Michael. Darcy was on days off from happy hour treating, Princess Sophia was sunning herself in PV, NellyBelle was back up working in Ft Mac, and the boys, well...

Matt and Luc were on Week Two of their mad affair, and Jonny was boycotting the bar as a result. "Fucking baby," as George put it. Adam had taken to hanging out with Jonny after work, playing video games and smoking pot.

God, Michael missed Matt. Missed being the cause of that giggle he giggled. Missed that flawless little bum. Missed kissing him. God, how he missed kissing him! Playful kisses. Passionate kisses. Peck on the lips or full out face-eating. All of the kissing, more than the sex, more than the mind-shattering orgasms...

"Quit daydreaming!" George barked. "My older sister Ralph and I need a sambuca!"

"Already?"

"Just you pour them and save the sass!"

"Do you let him talk to you like that?" Ralph asked Michael.

"Mom always taught me to respect my elders... and you can't get much elder than George!"

Ralph cackled "Oh, we like this one!"

"He's alright," George grudgingly admitted. "Too much drama though."

"Oh, you fucking love it, old man."

"You hush your face."

Bucas up, glasses down.

Shortly after, Matt and Luc came in, arms around each others waists. When Luc picked Matt up and swung him around and then kissed him, it was a dagger in the chest for Michael. Thank God this is only a short shift, he thought. Then Luc will be working and I won't have to stick around and watch this, god I miss those kisses!

At eight, Luc took over the till and Michael was off. As he put on his jacket, George barked, "where are you going? You never drink with your old friend George anymore!"

"I drank with you all day, old man! I'm going home!"

"Just one beer! Quick Luc, a beer for Michael."

"OK. Just one." The chairs were all full, save one next to Matt. Michael stood next to George.

One beer became two became three with shots. And then Michael was sitting next to Matt, and they were laughing, drinking, shooting. Oh sure, all the flirting and touching between Matt and Luc was still daggers, but those daggers were numbed now, by the beer, the 'buca, the blow.

"Let's go to the Underground," Matt said suddenly.

"What?"

"Come with me. I've never been."

"I'm not going to the baths with you."

"Maybe I'll suck your dick."

"Let's go!" Michael tipped back his beer and Matt tipped back his gin and they were into a cab and then they were checking in and then they were standing at their lockers and Matt was stripping and there was that wonderful Matt ass.

"Hurry up!" Matt said, wrapping a towel around his waist. He started undoing Michael's pants.

"Hey! I can do that!" Michael said, shooing Matt away, feeling his face flush, his dick plump.

Matt giggled his Matt giggle, as Michael stripped off, locked his locker, wrapped his towel around his waist. Matt groped Michael's dick through the towel. "K show me around."

What am I doing here, Michael thought.

What am I doing here, Michael thought, sitting in his mother's car outside of Divas, the only gay bar in Edmonton he knew of. He'd just needed a break from family and Easter and figured Greg was right, he could go by himself.

But now, sitting in front of the big brick building with its glowing neon Divas sign, he didn't want to go in. He was going to look like a loser, all by himself.

He's spent so much time being a loser by himself in grade school, back when we was "in love" with all the Taras and Heathers and Kalyns (probably overcompensating for popping wood over Kent he knew now). He wasn't used to being that high school loser anymore though. His apartment in Lethbridge had been Homo party central; people always called him to see what everyone was doing. He was out and happy and popular so what the fuck was he doing in a parked car outside a bar? Suck it up, and go inside and maybe find someone to suck it off.

OK, he'd been horny as much as bored. As amazing as the kissing and handjobs with Greg had been, he wanted dick in his ass and he wanted it now. And he wasn't going to get it in the car.

Into Divas Michael went, and it felt like home. A dance floor of flashing lights and disco divas (hey! Maybe that's where the name came from, he thought) and men so many men (and some lesbians but so many men). No different than Metro in Calgary (no, don't go there, Metro leads to Troy too easily). Oh look, a bar. Oh look, a drink. Oh look, a table.

And he sat and drank and watched so many men, and drank so many beers, and then oh look, tequila!

Tequila up, glass down.

"Shooters alone, hun?" It was a tall thin guy, kinda familiar...

"Excuse me?"

"It's Iona," he said, "Well, Darcy."

"Oh, haha, I didn't even recognize you."

"How are you, my dear?"

"Good thanks."

"Is Troy with you?"

"No, he moved to Toronto actually." And we'd broken up because of you, he added to himself. But, he figured it was someone to talk to anyway.

"And what brings you to my fair city?"

"Up for Easter. Family."

"Oh Easter! Such a lovely holiday, and oh! Look at the Easter basket on him!" he said, pointing out a passing crotch. "Shooter, my dear?"

"Sure."

They shot, they drank, Darcy showed him around, introduced him to a bevy of Queens (and their very attractive arm candy. Apparently, if the adorable Justin and the sexy Sean were any indication, there were advantages to dressing like a woman, Michael thought.

"Well I'm off though," Darcy suddenly said.

"So early? It's only midnight."

"Ah but it's the Easter egg hunt at Underground," he explained. "Why settle for bunnies with baskets when you can find someone hung like Jesus?"

Michael laughed. "Is that another bar?"

Darcy laughed. "Oh no my dear, it's the bathhouse next door."

"Never been to one."

"What? My dear boy, you're missing out!"

"Iona, you leave this chicken alone, you dirty old queen," one of the other queens said.

"It is the duty of the old to educate the young."

"Pervert."

"Oh Michael and I are old friends," Darcy said. "Besides, I like a man with a bit more meat on his bones." He grabbed Michael's crotch. "Not that your meat isn't plenty to make some young thing happy." He laughed. "Toodles all!"

Darcy walked off. Bathhouse? Michael thought. Really? Could be fun. Well maybe one more beer then maybe.

One beer became two became three, with shots, with his new drag queen acquaintances, who ignored him as politely as they could. Damn, Michael thought, it's after 2. I can't drive. Mom will kill me. Well, maybe I can hang out at this bathhouse 'til I sober up.

The fresh air hit him hard when he stepped outside. He looked down the street. Just a parking lot. Other way? Hmm maybe down this alley? I guess. Oh. There's a red U. For Underground? I guess.

He went down a flight of stairs and found a small window.

"Room or locker?" the man behind the window said.

"Sorry?"

"First time?"

"Yes."

The man sighed. "You rent a room or locker. It's for 12 hours."

"Room, I guess?"

"$18. Come on in."

A buzzer sounded and Michael opened the door next to the window. It was dark, moist. Men were wandering around in towels.

"You're in 303," the man said, hanging Michael a towel, condom, lube packets, and a key on a wrist bracelet. "Down that way, to the left. Have fun."

Every man he passed eyed him, some with interest, some dismissively. He felt awkward, uncomfortable... and a little turned on. In his room, he locked the door, caught his breath, then stripped off, and wrapping the towel around his waist, stepped gingerly back into the hallway.

The passing looks were more appraising, now he was undressed. Occasionally, the look would be accompanied by the brush of fingers and once, a grope to the crotch.

It was all kinds of men, hairy, smooth, fat, athletic, fresh-faced, silver-haired. Some lay in rooms, doors opened, rubbing themselves, eyes inviting. Some sat and watched. Michael stumbled upon a wet area almost by accident, and showered. Hot tub, sauna, ooh! A steamroom! Inside, the steam was so thick! He could hear people breathing, could feel the occasional foot or hand, bumping into him by accident (or not?), could hear the telltale slurp of a cocksucker in action. He felt his dick get harder. A hand went up his towel, wrapped around the boner. Michael got up and bolted back to his room.

He caught his breath again, but the hard-on didn't go away. He had no idea whose hand it had been. Could've been a hotty. Could've been a troll. Did it matter? Could he stick his dick in some anonymous random hole? It twitched in response.

Michael sure didn't feel drunk anymore but he wasn't going home. This was a whole new world, and wow, he'd been missing out.

Sitting in the hot tub at Underground with Matt added a new thrill to an old spot. Between working and hanging out there when he'd first moved back, Michael had rapidly become over the Underground.

But now, he just wanted to be over Matt, or under Matt. Inside Matt. Matt's eyes were darting about like a kid in a candy store (a really horny kid in a really naked candy store) but his excitement was obvious, and the sight of his erection bobbing in the water was enough to get Michael throbbing.

Michael gingerly let his foot bump Matt's under the water. They were naked, they were hard. Why weren't they fucking? Matt pulled away (a hard-on deflater if there ever was one).

"Let's go to the steamroom," Matt said, his eyes following a muscle bear into the steam.

"I'm good, you go though," Michael said, and Matt was out of the water, towel in hand, hard-on leading the way.

It wasn't going to happen, was it? Matt was over him. From the hot tub, Michael could sort of see into the steam room. Someone was on their knees, soles of their feet pressed against the glass. Was it Matt, blowing the muscle bear? The musclebear, blowing Matt? Someone else, going from Matt's cock to the musclebears as they kissed? Oh, sweet Matt kisses!

Snap out of it, Michael. Don't sit and watch. Go get some of your own.

Michael went into the sauna, glancing once over his back in case Matt was coming back for him. He wasn't. Someone had thrown a towel over the sauna light. In the pitch black, Michael could hear the grunts and moans and skin on skin sounds of sex. He felt his way to an empty spot. A hand on his thigh did little to arouse him even as the fingers played with his balls. The moaning grew louder. Moaning like Matt with Michael's dick inside him. Yes, that made him hard. It was Matt making those sounds, it was Matt's mouth wrapping around his dick. He closed his eyes tightly. Yes, it was Matt.

Bodies shifted and the light came on as whoever's towel it had been was reclaimed. It was not Matt.

Michael pulled his dick out of the mouthy of the scrawny Asian sucking it. He was soft again, in a towel and out of the sauna, into a hot shower. Cleansed, kinda, he went into the steamroom. It was empty.

So was he. Inside.

Michael never felt as full as he did when he had a dick inside him and that first night at Underground, he got fucked like he'd never been fucked before.

He was sitting in the hot tub, enjoying the heat, the occasional bit of eye candy. Most of the people were too old or too fat but he was mostly just wanting to sober up now. It was after 4. Another hour and he'd be good to drive home. Maybe he'd come back tomorrow night before he caught the midnight bus back to...

HOLY

SHIT

Into the wet area marched an absolute stud of a man, blond hair clipped short over bulging pecs, star tattoo around his belly button on his tight abs, and then his towel dropped to reveal an absolute ANACONDA of a penis, and this GOD was in the pool with Michael. His eyes were closed though. How to smile or make eye contact? Dammit!

And then suddenly, under the bubbles, Michael felt a foot rub his foot, and when he didn't pull his foot away, the GOD slid across the tub to Michael's side, took Michael's hand under the water, guided it to his rock hard ANACONDA (even bigger now).

"Do you have a room?" His voice was low, so low Michael barely heard.

"What? Oh. Yes."

"Want to go there?"

"OK." Michael gulped. They got out of the tub, water dripping off the Blond God that Michael suddenly felt so inferior next to, in every way.

The God followed Michael to his room. Michael fumbled with his keys. Inside, Michael sat down on the bed. The God took off his towel and was still fully erect. "Suck it."

Michael dropped to his knees. The God grabbed his head, fucking his face. Michael gagged a bit, hands clutching thighs like tree trunks. The God grunted, pulled Michael up by the underarms and turned him around. That ANACONDA was pressing up against him. Michael heard the tear of plastic, felt cold lube on his hole, felt one finger, two, then...

"Ah," he gasped out, falling forward onto the bed. His body tensed. He gasped again as a hand pushed him down onto the bed.

He didn't even know if it felt good or hurt. It was so big. Inside him it felt even bigger. On and on it went, and then the God pulled out. Michael gasped for air but it was only a reprieve. BAM! He was flipped onto his back, his legs pushed back, and this blond God was on him, in him, up him. Michael scrunched his eyes and began to moan. Whiskers rubbed his neck roughly. He turned his head, trying to find the stranger's mouth. Lips met, briefly, and then Michael felt it, liquid fire inside him as the man came.

Michael lay there, panting, as the man pulled out. "Thanks," he said, and grabbing his towel, was gone, leaving Michael alone there, an emptiness inside him, an empty lube, an unopened condom.

Michael couldn't breathe.

Michael couldn't breathe. Fucking coke. Fuck fuck. His whole body vibrated. I didn't even do that much, he thought! His chest was so tight. Fuck. Oh God. I hate this feeling. Why do I do this? Could a heart actually race like this and not explode? What a way to fucking die. Fuck God God fuck. Through the deep ragged breaths, Michael said out loud, "please please please I will never do it again. Just make this feeling go away."

He started to cry.

He started to cry. How could he have not made sure the guy wore a condom? He wasn't stupid. What the fuck was he doing in some dirty bathhouse getting fucked by some stranger anyway. Fuck. What if he'd caught something? What a way to fucking die. Fuck God God fuck. Through the deep ragged breaths, Michael said out loud, "please please please, I will never have sex again. Just make me be okay."

I'm not OK. This has to stop. And why? Just cuz the bathhouse was dead, just cuz Matt was off sucking cock, I come home and inhale a pile of blow, and now look at me, I'm freaking out.

"I'm freaking out, Genie," Michael said.

"You'll be home tomorrow. You can go get tested."

"Why am I so stupid?"

"I haven't figured that out yet."

"Don't make me laugh."

"Well, you can't just freak out for the next ten days."

"Who says?"

"I don't understand why you'd cheat on Greg anyway."

"Greg and I are just friends." It was kinda true, he thought, mostly.

"If you say so..."

"I just wish I'd never done it."

"Was he hot at least?"

"Oh god so hot, but who doesn't use a condom? Like really!"

"You really should have made sure."

"Thanks, Mom."

"What do you want me to say, Michael?"

"Tell me it will be alright."

"It will be alright."

"Liar."

It will be alright, Michael told himself. You're not having a heart attack. You'll be fine. And then stop this shit. You're too old for it, for one. And it's fucking up your life. Time to grow up. Quit that fucking bar. Clean start somewhere else. Where people don't know you're such a druggy loser. Then you'll find a great man and a white picket fence and oh God why won't my heart slow down. Please please please.

I'll never do it again.

Liar, Michael told himself, the next day. Well, it's just a small bump. Just to get me through my shift. Then it's home to bed. Then tomorrow, tomorrow, it's time to clean up my act.

"Sorry, Greg. Tomorrow, it's just school then home to study." After getting tested. "I have to study all week." And wait for my results. "I'll call you when I'm done finals." And when I know.

-Adam, want to grab some dinner when I'm off work tonight?-

-why, are Matt and Jonny going somewhere-

-no, just you and me-

-you're not going to want to stay and drink after work?-

-no, I promise-

-well text me when you're done. Maybe I'll be around-

-text you in a couple hours-

"Hi Greg. It's Michael."

"Oh hey, how did your tests go?"

"I passed them all with flying colors!"

"Good to hear."

"Yup!" You don't know the half of it, Michael thought, fucking lucky!

-Hi Mikey. Thought you were gonna text me when you were done work-

-yah thats what I figured Michael. Have fun-

-maybe you should delete my number while you're at it Michael-

"Hi Adam, it's Michael. Sorry I didn't text and I get you're mad at me, but it's not my fault. George had a heart attack."

There was no official start date, it just kind of happened. After that close call with the unsafe sex, Michael shied away from any physical contact. Which seemed to work with just-coming-out Greg. The mutual handjobs seemed forgotten, lost for Michael anyway in the steam and the panic of the ANACONDA.

But they hung out, every day, and maybe it was Genie's foresight, but one day in the fall, Michael turned to Greg and said "are we going out?"

"I think so," Greg said, his hands never stopping their backrub.

Working in construction for five years had given Greg rough callused hands that felt absolutely incredible on Michael's skin. It was that, even more than the pretty green eyes with fluttering black lashes that cemented it in Michael's head.

Greg made him feel good, and after all the drama with David and Cory and Troy (and ANACONDA), what was wrong with feeling good?

They'd cuddle during movies.

They'd go for dinner.

They'd have a quiet night in.

It was nice.

And 'nice' was a nice change.

Michael's lease was up at the end of October. That Thanksgiving, Greg asked, "do you want to get a place together? I'm tired of being in my parents' basement, and I'm here all the time anyway."

Moving in with a boyfriend? Wow. It hadn't occurred to Michael, maybe because the relationship was so asexual, maybe because he was so focused on this final semester.

"Yes," Michael said, "let's do it."

They found a cute little house to rent. A house! No white picket fence though. But still, if happiness can be found in four walls, Michael thought, I can find it here. As all their friends gathered for a housewarming, Michael saw a glimpse of a rosy future.

The PBC was full. Princesses of days gone by came out to hear the news first hand, and Michael thought, looking around the bar, that if happiness can be found in four walls, it was here. Michael, part newscaster, part gossip, all Princess, told them what they'd come to hear.

"He should be out of the hospital this weekend, but there's going to have to be some changes.

'No more smoking for sure, And," he paused for effect, "no more sambuca." This was met with groans (and a few cheers). "He's just carrying too much weight."

"Plus it can't be easy being such a cunt," LBP said, to a round of laughter.

"Who knew the old bastard had a heart to give out?" Darcy said, to a round of louder laughter.

"Cheers to George!" Michael said, to a round of sambuca.

Bucas up, glasses down.

To outsiders, the PBC may have seemed like a bunch of absolutely horrid queens, tearing each other down for cheap laughs and to make themselves feel better. To an extent, that was true. But only on the surface. Underneath that cunty exterior was genuine affection for each other that did surface when needed.

Like when Waldorf died.

Or when Princess Sophia's husband passed away from cancer.

Or when Darcy was being beat up by his boyfriend.

When life got too real, the PBC was there for each other with a warm hug, a cold shot, and a friendly smile. Some people say "I love you" with flowers. Some people say it with a song.

Sometimes people say "I love you" with a "fuck you, cunt".

Michael had already opened the bar and was gossiping with LBP when George came in. Michael stopped, mid joke, his throat catching.

George had aged ten years. His face was so gray! He moved slowly up to the bar, and lifted himself so slowly onto his stool.

"Uhm, sambuca please!"

"Nope. No sambuca for you."

"Is that right?" he barked. Well, half-barked.

"Yeah that's right. Do you wanna end up back in the hospital?"

"Fucking ugly nurses, no thank you."

"Water? Juice?"

"Uhm, sambuca."

"Not while I'm working." Michael poured him an orange juice. "Here. Juice up, glass down."

George sneered at it, then tossed it back. "Fuck I'm gorgeous!"

Michael and LBP laughed. "Oh, we missed you!"

"Fuck you, cunts!"

"I love you, you know," Greg told Michael.

"I know." He paused. "I love you too."

Greg kissed Michael softly on the neck, as they were spooning watching a movie. "It'll be weird not being with you at Christmas."

"Yah."

"You could always stay here."

"Mom would flip. You could always come with."

"I'd love to but I work. Besides, family is stressful enough without bringing home your boyfriend for the first time."

"True."

Greg's hands, those strong hands, wandered. "Someone's tense tonight.."

"Finals."

"Massage?"

"Sure." Greg's hand slid into Michael's pants, causing an instant reaction. "Hey!"

"What? You're all tense."

"Are you sure?" Greg took Michael's hand and put it on his crotch. His dick twitched. "Yes, I guess you're sure."

They undressed themselves slowly. Sure, they saw each other naked all the time but that was it. Greg had always kaiboshed anything further. Greg went down on Michael first. Oh it had been too long! He flipped around so he could repay the favor.

Greg let out a moan. "Oh yah," Michael said, "I guess that's your first blowjob." He went back to sucking.

It didn't take either of them long to come.

"Well, that was fun," Greg said.

"Yah, it was nice." Just nice, Michael thought, forcing a smile.

Michael forced a smile. "Hi, Jonny."

"Hi."

It was awkward, just the two of them in the bar. "Your usual?"

"Yah." Michael prepped the drink. "Look Michael," Jonny said at the same time as Michael said, "Ok Jonny..."

"You first."

"This is stupid, Jonny. Can't we go back to normal?"

"I'd like to. You're right. This is dumb."

"It's not like there's anything going on between me and Matt."

"Anymore anyway."

"Yes, anymore."

"And I did get to fuck you first," Jonny said, grinning.

"Yes you did."

"Maybe I should get another go."

"Maybe," Michael said. "Shooter?"

Michael smiled. "Hey, Adam."

"Hi. Look Michael, I am so sorry about those texts. I feel like such an ass."

"Is that why you've been avoiding me?"

"Well yah, I just feel..."

Michael put a finger up to Adam's lips. "Shhh!" It was the first time he'd felt Adam's mouth. His finger went across Adam's cheek, down his jaw, his chest. He pictured tangling his hand in Adam's curls, pulling him in with his belt, a frenzied first kiss "It's all good."

Adam grinned, dopily. "So how you been?"

"I've been better, let's be honest. But it's ok."

"I was worried about you. I know how close you and George are."

"He's been my boss for a long time."

"And your friend."

"And my friend," Michael nodded and he suddenly felt his eyes brim with tears. It would be easy to fall against Adam right now, to seek comfort, to feel his body. "But I'm ok."

Adam put his hand on Michael's shoulder. "If you need to talk..." Michael's hand held Adam's there."

"I know. Thank you."

Their eyes met. Fire. Energy. Goosebumps. And then "Adam I..." at the same time as "Michael I...." and then BAM.

Michael remembered every detail about his first kiss with Kevin Kosinski. He knew exactly what Troy was wearing the first night they kissed. He could still smell Matt's cologne from their first kiss.

Later on, he'd not be able to remember anything about that first kiss with Adam. His senses all disappeared into the moment. It was foot-popping and fireworks and Michael broke away from it with a smile that started in his chest.

It was right.

It wasn't right.

Nice didn't cut it.

He'd always known, Michael guessed. Just didn't want to admit it.

security, stability, comfort, they seemed to count for more than passion.

But as he stared out the Greyhound window into the lightly falling snow, he was dreading the return to Lethbridge, to the rut.

As nice as it had been.

Maybe it was finishing school and finally being done.

Maybe it was setting foot in a gay bar for the first time in nine months and remembering how much he loved the lights, the music, the men (so many men).

But how could he do this to Greg?

Greg was so nice.

It would crush him.

If Michael did that, took Greg's heart and smashed it on the floor, all those people who'd called him an asshole or drama queen or a user over the years would be right.

Did he care? He was done school, he could be done with this city, with its shades of David and Cory and Troy. (And go where? Home to Edmonton where crazy mothers and barebacking anaconda dicks offered all new dramas?)(Or to Calgary with its lights and its music and its men (so many men) and all their own dramas?)

Michael was tired of the drama, and that's what had been so nice.

It makes for a long and lonely bus ride, he thought, and what's waiting for me at home?

What was waiting was what he didn't expect and exactly what he needed.

Adam was everything Michael needed, and it was what he'd never expected.

Through George sitting there, still gray, and back on the 'buca, and now randomly dozing off at the PBC...

Through the binge drinking blackouts getting progressively more frequent, even with the sobering bumps of coke...

Through the spurts of heart-racing terror from coke binges that kept him up...

Through all of it, Adam was there.

Well, emotionally there. He left before the drinking got too out of control, and Michael always held off on the coke while Adam was around.

Almost always, anyway.

"And how's the sex? That's what I want to know," Darcy said, one Friday as they were partaking of a late night treat.

Michael sniffed long and loud, Iona-sized after all. "It's amazing Darcy."

"Big dick?"

"Beautiful dick." He'd known that already of course, from Matt, who had no qualms about sharing any and every intimate detail no matter how clearly painful those details were to hear. Adam, on the other hand, was a whole lot less forthcoming, for which Michael was grateful.

"It's only been a couple times. There's been so much going on."

"How are things around here?"

"Quiet."

"How's George?"

"He's the quiet part. It's weird."

"You can't party that long without consequences," Darcy said, "how's my nose?"

"You got a little something."

He wiped. "Better?"

"Yes. Me?"

"Good. Let's go."

It was nearly midnight, and Michael looked around with an expression of "this is it?" on his face. Princess Sophia and NellyBelle cackling at the bar, Matt and Jonny dancing, some lesbians playing pool. The DJ was playing games on his iPad.

"Rocking Friday."

"Isn't it though?"

"I'm going home, I think. Do you want the rest?"

"No, you take it. I think Adam's coming back. Don't want cokedick."

"OK, cheers my dear boy." Darcy kissed Michael's cheek and stumbled down the hall.

Michael sat down in George's spot. His body tingled from the blow. He had to stop though. If not for his health, for Adam. It's weird, he thought, how someone can be on the periphery of your life for so long and then suddenly take centre stage.

Matt who? Jonny who? He smiled. Matt and Jonny would be together forever. The Luc phase had fizzled and now it was just them.

"Can I get another one, Michael?"

"Sure, Princess."

As Michael poured just one more for Rick, Rick said, "I feel really bad about what I said."

"Weeks ago. Don't worry about it."

"Still, it wasn't my place."

"You were worried about me. I know it's stupid. Here's your drink. I know I need to stop."

"I need to stop this."

"But not tonight?"

"But not tonight."

"Same."

"One day."

"Some day."

"Soon."

"Probably."

"Probably." Rick nodded.

"Cheers."

"Cheers, Michael."

-Cheers Michael- The postcard read. -Hope you have an awesome Christmas. You're all done school now hey? Congrats. Life in TO is awesome. It was hard to leave but glad I did. You have to come visit. This city is awesome. Taking chances pays off, no matter how scary. Luv ya, Troy-

That postcard waiting for him when he got home, it was a sign. He picked up the phone.

"Hey, Mom. Made it back safe."

"What's wrong?"

Uncanny. "How'd you know?"

"Little birdy told me. Mothers always know."

"I could move home right?"

"Sure... why?"

"I just don't know if I'm happy here, and now that school's done..."

"What about your friend?" That's all Greg ever was to her, and maybe, just maybe, that's all he had ever been to Michael..

"We'd probably have to break up."

"He wouldn't want to move with you?"

"I don't think I'd ask him to."

"You have to do what's best for you, Michael. This is always your home of course."

"Thank you."

"We love you, son."

"Love you too, Mom."

Now just to tell Greg, Michael thought. Oh God I hope there's no drama. How can there not be drama!

As Michael waited for Greg to get home, he looked around the house. There weren't any painful memories, it was all perfectly pleasant. Nothing really stood out though. Day in, day out, same thing. School for Michael and work for Greg. Home, dinner, TV, cuddle, bed, repeat.

Months of it.

When he moved already (already it was 'when' not 'if'), he'd have a whole great big gayborhood at his fingertips. Maybe he'd get a job at Divas; he could handle being a bartender, for a while anyway.

It wasn't about finding a different guy, it really wasn't, Michael told himself. But maybe, there on the dance floors of the big city, he'd find someone with the sweetness of David, the passion of Cory, the romance of Troy, the security of Greg, all in one guy (with an anaconda dick?)

"You home, Michael?"

"In the bedroom," he called. Here goes, he thought, and breathed deep.

Greg came in. "How was your trip?" Hug. Quick kiss. Nice

"It was nice."

"Nice"

"Yah... so there's no nice way to say this. I think I want to move home."

"What? When?"

"Soon."

"Oh... what does that mean about us?"

"Well it would be pretty hard to have such a long distance relationship"

"Are you asking me to go with you?"

Deep breath. "No."

"Oh." Pretty green eyes were teary behind dark lashes. "So are we breaking up?"

"I think so." You're not a nice guy Michael. Not at all. "I'm sorry."

"Me too, Michael. Me too."

Pretty green eyes filled with devastation. I caused that, Michael thought, starting to cry. "I'm really sorry."

"It was nice while it lasted," Greg said.

Nice!

"Mmm that was nice," Michael said, rolling off Adam and onto his back.

"Very nice," Adam said, propping himself up on an elbow and kissing Michael.

"I'm glad you came down tonight."

"Me too. It's good you and Rick made up."

"And me and Jonny."

"And you and Jonny," Adam agreed. "So did you do any blow tonight?"

"Honestly? A little."

"Thanks for being honest."

"I'm almost ready to quit though."

"Good. I'll be glad when you do."

"Me too."

"So do it."

"Soon."

"OK." Adam kissed Michael again, rolled over. "Good night Michael"

"Good night Adam."

The light from the car dealership across the way brightened up the room. Michael traced the light as it fell on Adam's back. Adam moaned softly and shifted into his sleeping position, legs wrapped around a pillow. So adorable, Michael thought. I think I really love this guy.

They hadn't said it yet though. Michael wouldn't be the first. How many times had he said it? To how many guys? Love had to be more than the thrill of something new. More than the lust of the moment

He'd thought he loved Matt. Not so long ago at that. Now he could see it for the borderline obsession it was. Who'd been before that? There'd been Todd, a couple years ago, but that was a dysfunctional drugged up mess. Before that, fuck, there'd been tricks. One night stands. Drunken bathhouse fucks. Nothing that was close to love.

Oh, there'd been Dan, not too long after he moved here. That was sweet. Not love though. Just adjustment to a new city. Where was Dan now? Where were all the people he'd met when he moved here? Lost in the crowd, the lights, the music, the men (so many men).

Just a corner filled with princesses and one cranky old buzzard squawking for sambuca.

A key full of coke.

And Adam.

Michael leaned down, kissed Adam on the shoulder. "I love you," he said.

Half-asleep, Adam moaned, "Mmm that's nice." And then started to snore.

Michael chuckled. Nice!

It was busy for a Monday, which was, Michael thought, nice. Little Buddy Pump and Darcy and NellyBelle, Princess Sophia and Statler, Matt and Jonny and this new kid Ben (who they were both fucking apparently).

A Princess Bar filled with Princesses, and Michael served up rounds of drinks and shots to the percussive laugh and cough of George, perched there on his corner, king of all he surveyed.

The door opened and heads turned. "Here comes trouble!" George yelled. "Come, lay it on the bar and make an old man happy. I'll buy you a drink for every inch!" He slammed his hand on the bar. "Ha! You'll owe me money!" He laughed, coughed, laughed. "Round of sambucas!"

-I'm getting treats. Want some?-

Michael texted Darcy back -I'm good thanks- He smiled at Adam, who smiled back, knowingly.

"Hi babe," Michael said, kissing Adam across the bar.

"Isn't that fucking cute?" LBP said.

"Jealous much?"

"Not me. I had afternoon delight with a hot black daddy."

"Did you take pictures?"

"Dirty old troll!"

"Those who can't do, watch!"

"That should be your slogan, Princess Sophia!"

"Unless Ho Chi Minh's in town!" George barked. "Round of sambucas!"

"So Matt," Michael said, as he poured the round, "where'd you find this chicken?"

"Grindr. Jealous?"

"Not at all," Michael said, smiling at Adam.

"Ok bitches!" George yelled. "Belly up to the bar. Here's to big cocks!"

Bucas up, glasses down.

"You're probably done hey?" Michael said to George.

"I'm done when I say I'm done."

"Just sayin'."

Michael cleared up the glasses, wiped down the bar.

"He's dozed off already," LBP whispered.

"Fuck, I'll call him a cab."

Michael dialed, ordered, shook George. "Where's my drink?" he barked.

"Right there, you silly old troll."

"Fuck, I'm gorgeous!"

"You sure are, George," Darcy said.

"I want someone pretty," he snapped. Laughed. Coughed.

Michael, through the door, saw a taxi pull up.

"George, your cab's here."

"Humph. Fuck you cunts." And he stumbled off down the hall. They watched him go. Watched him get into the cab slowly. The cab drove off.

"Anyone for a sambuca?" Michael said. He was met by a chorus of NO.

"George passed away in his sleep at home, which is a lot better than in a pool of spilled sambuca like so many of us joked, George included. I used to dread coming in to open the bar and finding hm. Now, I dread going in and not finding him.

'Let's be honest. He was an asshole. Yes, laugh, you're allowed. He was an asshole but an asshole that loved to laugh. I have never met anyone who had such a zest for life. Never met anyone who could make someone feel so welcome with a grunt. Never met anyone who loved sambuca so much.

'We're all here to say goodbye to a very dear friend. In spite of how angry he made us sometimes, let's be honest. He made us angry because he was right. He knew how things work, and why, and sure his delivery sucked but his heart was gold.

'Well 3/4 gold, 1/4 Luxardo.

'I remember when I first met George. I'd just moved back here from Lethbridge, just broken up with my boyfriend to come try life here. I got hired at Underground and met George and he brought me here and I met all of you, and George told me something that day that I've never forgotten.

'These people, they're bitches, he said, they'll lie and gossip and they'll cause drama and you'll hate them. And they're the best friends you will ever have because when the bottle is empty, they'll still be there.

'He was so right.

'So many times, he was right. I wish he was here so I could thank him for being right. And thank him for being such an asshole.

'OK bitches.

'Bucas up.

'Glasses down.

'Fuck I'm gorgeous."

LAST CALL

(aka the end)

EPILOGUE

The phone rang, and Michael debated not answering it. It had been a long day, with the funeral, and the booze that followed the funeral, and the hot Adam sex that followed the booze following the funeral, and really, who would be calling at nearly midnight?

"Hello?" he said, quietly so as not to wake Adam.

"Hey, is this Michael?"

"Yes, who's this?"

"I don't think we've ever actually met. This is Jim Taylor. I'm the owner of Divas."

"I know who you are. No, we haven't met. What's up?"

"I hope I didn't call you too late. I got your phone number from your friend, Jonny. First, I wanted to offer you my condolences. I know you worked for George for a long time."

"Thank you."

"I know you probably haven't even given much thought to what happens next, but something has come up here, and I wanted to see if you were interested. I know the timing isn't good at all." The voice paused. "Or, actually, very good, as the case may be, just bad circumstances."

"I'm afraid I'm not following you."

"Could you come down and meet tomorrow afternoon? I think this might be easier in person."

"What's this about?"

"Well, to not beat around the bush, my manager has left, and I thought maybe you would like to fill the position. I don't know what will be happening with Choices, now that George has passed, but I think there's a tremendous opportunity for us here, to build something wonderful for Edmonton's gay community. "

"I - I don't even know what to say."

"Say you'll come down and meet tomorrow. Say 3 pm?"

"Ok. See you at 3."

"Sorry, again, for your loss. See you tomorrow."

Michael hung up. Adam stirred next to him. "What was that about?" he asked, half asleep.

"The future."

PARALLEL LIVES

About the Author

Rob Browatzke (born 1977) is a proud Edmontonian, a proud homosexual, and a proud writer. This is his second published novel.

Feel free to stalk him on social media.

Made in the USA
San Bernardino, CA
20 January 2018